A HARD HEART

THE EARLY HOURS
OF A REVILED MAN

PLAYSCRIPT 119

A HARD HEART

THE EARLY HOURS OF A REVILED MAN

Howard Barker

CALDER PUBLICATIONS · RIVERRUN PRESS
London · Paris · New York

First published in Great Britain in 1992 by
Calder Publications Ltd
9–15 Neal Street, London WC2H 9TU

and in the United States of America in 1992 by
Riverrun Press Inc
1170 Broadway, New York, NY 10001

All performing rights in these plays are strictly reserved and no performance may
be given unless a licence has been obtained prior to rehearsal. Applications for a
licence should be made to:

Judy Daish Associates Ltd, 83 Eastbourne Mews, London W2 6LQ.

British Library Cataloguing in Publication Data
Barker, Howard
    Hard Heart AND Early hours of a reviled man. -
    (Playscript Series; No. 119).
    I. Title II. Barker, Howard III. Series
    822.914

ISBN 0-7145-4228-8

Library of Congress Cataloging in Publication Data
Barker, Howard.
    A hard heart & The early hours of a reviled man two plays / by
    Howard Barker
    88 p. 19.8 cm.
    ISBN 0-7145-4228-8 (paper)
    I. Barker, Howard. Early hours of a reviled man. II. Title.
PR6052. A6485H37 1992   91-4636
822′ .912--dc20   CIP

Typeset in 9/10 pt Times by Pure Tech Corporation, Pondicherry, India
Printed in Great Britain by Hillman Printers (Frome) Ltd, Frome, Somerset

CONTENTS

A HARD HEART

CHARACTERS

RIDDLER	A Woman of Originalty
PRAXIS	The Queen of a City
ATTILA	A Son of Riddler
PLEVNA	A Military Commander
SEEMORE	A Vagrant
SENTRY	Riddler's Guard
A WOMAN	In a Crowd
SECOND WOMAN	In a Crowd

Scene I

A room in a palace. The distant effect of violence.

RIDDLER: Privacy. (*Pause*)
PRAXIS: Not any more. (*Pause*)
RIDDLER: I must have it.
PRAXIS: The first casualty of
RIDDLER: I must
PRAXIS: Strife
RIDDLER: Have it
PRAXIS: Siege
RIDDLER: No matter what I must. (*Pause. Distant effects.*)
  Also silence. (*Laughter*)
PRAXIS: Equally
RIDDLER: Yes
PRAXIS: Preposterous
RIDDLER: And thirdly
PRAXIS: Equally
RIDDLER: Manners. (*Pause*)
PRAXIS: Are you rebuking me for
RIDDLER: I must have silence. I must have solitude. I require to
  be addressed in tones which are respectful and preserve a proper
  distance. I need to feel the space that lies between myself and
  others is inviolable, a channel of perfect seclusion, the proximity
  of others bruises me, I am offended by uninvited intimacy, I
  know the city is under siege but some things can be preserved
  or else defence is pointless, defence of what if not of civil
  virtues, those are my terms and it is nothing to me if you think
  me absurd what you call absurdity is culture in my eyes you see
  how cleanly I have dressed for this interview though I know my
  clothing does not interest you and scented my body though my
  body is not the object of your need, but I required these things
  even to speak, and my son must not be drafted into the army.
  (*Pause*)
PRAXIS: Impossible
RIDDLER: He's frail
PRAXIS: Listen
RIDDLER: He gets appalling colds and the shortage of fruit
PRAXIS: I can't concede
RIDDLER: Makes him

PRAXIS: I won't concede
RIDDLER: Even more susceptible in fact he has not been free of
PRAXIS: **You know I can't** (*Pause*)
RIDDLER: Infection all this winter (*Pause*) I don't entreat you I insist (*Pause*)
PRAXIS: How terrible is this appetite for privilege. How relentless this hunger for
RIDDLER: Yes (*Pause*)
PRAXIS: You make me ashamed (*Pause*). Hide him in your house and if he steps into the street
RIDDLER: Of course
PRAXIS: **You make me a party to injustice at a time when**
RIDDLER: Sacrifices should be shared? (*Pause*)
 I am lending my mind to the city. I am lending my imagination, which is not a reservoir of bottomless depth but a thing wrenched out of steel, hammered in the hours of waking and also in sleep, I am yielding to the city the quickest intellect within its boundaries. I don't exaggerate or why did you ask me here, I am yoking the freedom and promiscuity of my thought to the service of the State, give me a little thing in exchange. I may save everyone from death even the lowest lout or beggar's mongrel let alone the galleries of art, give me my somewhat idle son, an unimpressive fragment of our culture for whom I entertain these incomprehensible feelings of love I do not think he even reciprocates illogical but compelling I am a realist and so are you, don't marshall more arguments or proper indignation it falls on deaf ears. (*Pause*)
PRAXIS: They are building a wall at right angles to ours.
RIDDLER: Yes.
PRAXIS: They are less than a hundred yards away how are we to counter it?
RIDDLER: I don't know yet
PRAXIS: When will you know we are on the verge of
RIDDLER: I'll put my mind to it
PRAXIS: Quickly if you would if they make a breach it's death to all of us sons included, do I sound sarcastic I don't intend to be, or do I
RIDDLER: I need the silence I referred to.
PRAXIS: I'll have straw laid on the pavements.
RIDDLER: Yes and ban all traffic.
PRAXIS: What traffic, there is none.
RIDDLER: And there are children in neighbouring houses.
PRAXIS: They'll be removed.
RIDDLER: Some vagrant plays an instrument.
PRAXIS: Where?
RIDDLER: On the corner, several times I've asked him to
PRAXIS: I'll see he's shifted and the area roped off with tapes
RIDDLER: Thank you

PRAXIS: With officers
RIDDLER: Yes if you've some to spare
PRAXIS: **Their wall is twenty feet above our own**
RIDDLER: I know I did the measurements
PRAXIS: You did? (*Pause*)
  You did, did you? (*Pause. Effects of battery.*) We have no allies
  and everything is running out. Who would have thought in this
  age and we were so conciliatory all things we and our ancestors
  struggled to our habits are pacific now and (*Pause*)
RIDDLER: I've been under siege all my life. (*Pause*) I've built
  walls since I was a child. (*Pause*) I've stockpiled my emotions
  and consumed the zoo in my extremity. (*Pause*) Not happy obviously and yet. (*Pause*) At the edge of catastrophe you are so
  trembling and acute it is a sort of love it is an ecstasy of sorts I
  have two solutions to the wall and now I must make the drawings **I am not nice am I but you need me so**.

Scene 2

A house in the city.

ATTILA: What a perfect child I was...
RIDDLER: Yes...
ATTILA: Petulant but loving. Precocious but not without charm
  and the petulance caused by insatiable desire, don't you think?
RIDDLER: Yes...
ATTILA: Desire to make, desire to act, I was adult in ambition
  but infant in capacity, no wonder I was difficult and naturally I
  claimed attention.
RIDDLER: I gave it to you.
ATTILA: I was forever in your bed and you, it must be said,
  encouraged me.
RIDDLER: Did I?
ATTILA: Did I! Did I indeed! You encouraged me in every little
  vice and if I am imperfect it must be laid at your door and no
  one else's. Discipline there was, but spasmodic and what earned
  me a beating one day invited indulgent laughter on the next.
RIDDLER: Yes. I've never had the patience for consistency.
ATTILA: I was warped by you. Maimed by you. Disfigured, mo-
  rally, it might be said, and have been obliged to labour under
  such deformities of character it is no wonder I (*A ruler falls to
  a tiled floor. Pause.*)
  I don't think you are listening to me.
RIDDLER: I am listening. (*With enthusiasm.*) Now I will teach
  you something.

ATTILA: I don't want to be taught. I want to be heard! (*Pause*)
Always you loved work. Work, you loved, and I, sweet little
infant, was merely a diversion, a rapidly diminishing attraction
you put down like a tool. That's enough charm. That's enough
innocence. You shelve everyone. (*Pause*)

RIDDLER: I don't deny a single one of your assertions. And
it's perfectly true my mind is elsewhere. It always was. Even
at the heights and depths of intimacy I was, in part at least,
absent.

ATTILA (*petulantly*): Then you must love better! It is a duty to
love, and an obligation on all parents! I had a small breakdown
this morning by the way. I was crying and I couldn't stop. I'll
pick up the ruler, don't you do it. I will, how nice your shoes
are, the heels are just right for your posture —

RIDDLER: It's all right, they don't want you for the army. (*Pause.
The ruler is replaced.*)

ATTILA: Oh? (*Pause*)

RIDDLER: They can manage without you, I am assured. (*Pause*)
Kiss me, little one... (*Pause*)

ATTILA: And I am supposed to show you gratitude, am I?

RIDDLER: I don't know, kiss me...

ATTILA: I am to be impressed that you can stop the mechanism
of the State by muttering your name. **Who asked you to intervene!** (*Pause*)
No wonder I am childish. I am kept childish by your actions
which **Thank you thank you thank you** I could not have stood
the smell the bodies in the barracks and the language the coarse
language as for the uniforms

RIDDLER: Your skin would

ATTILA: I haven't the skin for the army.

RIDDLER: The skin alone

ATTILA: Disqualifies me

RIDDLER: That's what I said. Kiss me. (*A brief pause.*)
Let me tell you how an enemy is frustrated.

ATTILA: Yes!

RIDDLER: And then I must draw.

ATTILA: Yes.

RIDDLER: Without impediment.

ATTILA: I'll — (*Pause. He laughs.*) I'll do something!

RIDDLER: What?

ATTILA: I don't know yet. Something. How is an enemy frustrated? Say! (*Pause*)

RIDDLER: Really, you are useless, aren't you? Attila? I should
close my heart to you. (*Pause*)

ATTILA: Please, mother, don't. (*Pause. A noise of battle.*)

RIDDLER: Always, the enemy has an object on which he concentrates his energy. This object, the more passion he expends on
it, the more magnetic it becomes. In a sense, the object infatu-

ates the army, which sheds its critical intelligence for this disabling love. And as with all consuming passion, the lover, for all his vehemence, has never been more weak. What is the object of the enemy's desire? (*Pause*) Attila? (*Pause*)

ATTILA: The city.

RIDDLER: No. The wall.

ATTILA: The wall, yes!

RIDDLER: For whilst his first ambition was to seize the city, his efforts are now wholly directed against the wall.

ATTILA: Yes! That's so because they've built a wall to meet our wall and we —

RIDDLER: Are raising our wall to —

ATTILA: Compensate us and —

RIDDLER: God knows where it will stop. (*Pause*) Clearly the wall has taken possession of their minds.

ATTILA: And ours!

RIDDLER: Ours also, yes. (*Pause*)

ATTILA: So...
   How is an enemy frustrated?

RIDDLER: Think.

ATTILA: I am thinking. (*Pause*)
   No, I don't —

RIDDLER: Please, Attila, use your —

ATTILA: **I am using my mind, Mother, it is simply not** (*He sobs*)

RIDDLER: Oh, shh... shh...

ATTILA: Adequate...

RIDDLER: It is, forgive me, it is adequate, it is more more than adequate and I — (*He sobs*) I am —

ATTILA: It is so hard to be your son —

RIDDLER: I know —

ATTILA: Your only, only son —

RIDDLER: Hard, yes, horribly hard. **You make the object worthless, that is how**. (*Pause*) You render the thing so wanted a perfect nullity. You make the love-object vile. All that he seeks becomes ash in his mouth, as a man seduced by so much effort can appear, in the cold light of a morning, a comic rebuke to love itself... (*Pause*)

ATTILA: You mean, give up the wall? (*A sound of construction.*)

Scene 3

Part of the city walls.

PRAXIS: As you instructed us, we have hung great cloths on poles, behind which our activities are invisible.

RIDDLER: Excellent.

PRAXIS: Of course they have tried to set fire to the cloths.

RIDDLER: Obviously

PRAXIS: But chains of buckets keep the cloths wet, as you recommended. Behind the cloths, the new wall is progressing.

RIDDLER: So I see

PRAXIS: When it is complete, we will cease wetting the cloths.

RIDDLER: Good.

PRAXIS: The cloths will dry and consequently —

RIDDLER: They will catch fire.

PRAXIS: The enemy will be delighted. But as the fire consumes the screen, they will see, looming through the smoke and laughter, not the satisfying spectacle of a wall conquered but a wall abandoned behind which —

RIDDLER: Lies another.

PRAXIS: Consequently, they will experience —

RIDDLER: Despair. Frustration. Bitterness. The appalling sense of an inferiority which saps the will and turns the men against their officers. Promises fade. Loot vanishes. The speech writers scrape their minds for phrases. As soon as the labourers are free we move to the construction of the engine. Visit me, I have the drawings. (*She makes to go.*)

PRAXIS: I — (*Pause*)
You are always in such a hurry — (*Pause*)
Always —

RIDDLER: Yes, I hate to stop and gossip, even with a monarch. Our platitudes might bar an idea, like silt closes a harbour even to the most necessary cargoes... (*Pause*)

PRAXIS: This wall. This new wall. Is made entirely out of houses.

RIDDLER: Yes. We cannot reach our quarries.

PRAXIS: It is made of houses and the winter's coming on. (*Pause*)

RIDDLER: Those whose houses are now walls must share the houses which remain. That is surely —

PRAXIS: They don't like sharing houses —

RIDDLER: Obvious to anyone.

PRAXIS: The rich, for example, don't like the poor.

RIDDLER: That is understandable. The poor don't like the rich also, but these little wars must be suspended in the interests of our survival as a culture, they can hate each other later.

PRAXIS: Perhaps you'd give a room —

RIDDLER: Of course not —

PRAXIS: To house some of the children —

RIDDLER: Of course not —

PRAXIS: We emptied out the orphanage? (*Pause*)

RIDDLER: No. Let the kind do that. (*She turns to go.*)

PRAXIS: The kind are in short supply!

RIDDLER: That's because the orphans are not sufficiently vociferous. Tell them to wail louder.

PRAXIS: I do think you are so —

RIDDLER: I think —

PRAXIS: So adamantine and impermeable to —

RIDDLER: I think —

PRAXIS: Pity or to conscience I —

RIDDLER: I think you are infringing the rule of manners we so —

PRAXIS: Yes —

RIDDLER: And privacy we so scrupulously —

PRAXIS: Yes —

RIDDLER: Erected —

PRAXIS: I admit it. I admit it! (*Pause*)
And I — frigidly — apologize... (*Pause.* RIDDLER *returns to* PRAXIS.)

RIDDLER: Listen. I am the best defence they have against their executions. The best, and you know it. Who cares about my character? Who stoops to smear their saviour with her faults? (*Pause*) I must go. It is too noisy here to think. (*She turns to go. Stops again.*) Do you ever wonder if they have a genius out there? Or are we supremely advantaged? It's obvious I am worth whole divisions. They outnumber us, but how inferior they feel. Their engineers are laborious, leaden, and everything they conceive of is immediately countered by us.

PRAXIS: By you.

RIDDLER: By me, yes. My single brain. My grey muck in its shell. All that stands between you and oblivion. Between the orphans and the axe. They will plough this place into the ground and plant thistle here, they've said so. (*Pause*)

PRAXIS: Obviously, you must not die. And when the food runs out, you must have the final crust... (*Sound of construction.*)

Scene 4

RIDDLER's *house. Out of the residue of noise, a single knocking on the door. The petulant slide of a window.*

RIDDLER: I am not to be disturbed. The city has granted me silence as a privilege.

SEEMORE (*below*): Let me in, then.

RIDDLER: Of course not. Who are you?

SEEMORE: I don't know who I am

RIDDLER: You don't know who you are? Look on your ration book. And don't pester me again. Those white tapes are the frontiers of my privacy.

SEEMORE: I don't know who I am since I laid eyes on you. (*Pause*)

RIDDLER: Oh, God, it is a madman...

ATTILA (*joining her*): Who's at the door, Mother?

RIDDLER: A man with a bald head. On the bald head is a scar through which his senses fled.

SEEMORE: **Come on or I will kick the door down**.

RIDDLER (*To* ATTILA): Bar the door if it's not done already. And look out for a policeman. (*A roar from below.*)

This is just the sort of thing that wrecks your concentration!

ATTILA: Suppose he kicks the door just at the moment I am reaching for the bar —

RIDDLER: Just do it! I will keep him talking.

ATTILA (*alarmed*): He's banging!

RIDDLER: Do it, I said! (*She leans out the window.*)

There is a soup kitchen half a mile down —

SEEMORE: **Don't want soup**.

RIDDLER: You don't? Then you're the only person who doesn't —

SEEMORE: **It's you I want**. (*Pause*)

No one is hungry who's in love. (*Pause*)

RIDDLER: That's the solution, then, to the food crisis...

ATTILA (*entering*):Can't see a policeman anywhere!

RIDDLER: There must have been an attack... (*She puts her head out.*) I have vital work to do and you are preventing me...!

SEEMORE: And my love, is that not vital, too? Let me in. I will sit as quiet as a bird on your desk, my head to one side slightly, following all your moves...

RIDDLER: No.

SEEMORE: And sing a little like a —

RIDDLER: No.

SEEMORE: **You shouldn't carry your body like that if you do not want attention!** (*Pause*)

RIDDLER: What?

SEEMORE: What, she says... you transport your body like it was a rare thing out of a museum... and standing, you place it like an exhibition, the rare property of an antique race. I saw this and I thought, she values it so highly I must be the thief. **You wanted to be stolen, confess**.

RIDDLER: When did you see me? I've never seen you.

SEEMORE: On the walls, of course, when you came to supervise the strategy. You leaned like this. You posed. You mannequin among engineers. And I am very violent, I am like the bells on the alarm posts, a single step sets me ringing. **Intruders in my peace, invaders of my habit!** (*Pause*) I was all right before I saw you. I knew who I was.

RIDDLER: And... who were you...? Before me?

SEEMORE: Another genius. (*Pause*)

RIDDLER: What a pity. But I hate to quarrel, so —

SEEMORE: **I love to quarrel**.
   With a bitch like you...

RIDDLER: Policeman! Over there! Wave!

ATTILA: I can't!

RIDDLER: Wave, I said!

ATTILA: I mustn't be seen!

RIDDLER (*calling*): Hey! (*A rattle.*)

ATTILA: He's gone! Quick as a silverfish in the lamplight!

RIDDLER: The city is all hiding places now... (*She slides the window.*)
   That's that.
   Silly interruption.
   Over

ATTILA: You can work now.

RIDDLER: Yes.
   Thank God. (*The pencil moves on the desk. The ruler. The stool.*)

ATTILA: How terrible things are in a siege. How we deteriorate. And the first thing to go is manners. Morals after that, and then the jokes become obscene, I don't think we can last, do you? Why don't we surrender? (*Silence of disbelief.*)
   I ask that
   I state that question
   In a purely theoretical
   Only theoretically
   Why? (*Pause*)

RIDDLER: I like the siege. (*Pause*)

ATTILA: You —

RIDDLER: Like it, yes.

ATTILA: But people are —

RIDDLER: Dying, yes, I am telling you the truth, I am honouring you who possibly does not deserve it, honouring you with such a savage honesty, **I like it**. It has nourished me like the sun falling on an ancient tomb might stir a seed to life after the silent centuries. I germinate. Dear child of my idle hours, I compliment you with my sincerity... (*Pause*)

ATTILA: Then... it follows... correct me if I'm wrong... you would not welcome a peace treaty...? (*Pause*)

You see, the elders say the enemy will execute the entire population, but I doubt that, the leaders, yes, them they'll give over to dreadful deaths, but not the young, surely, we have a certain value and (*Pause*)

Their culture, though it is so very different from ours (*Pause*)

Might be studied and (*Pause*)

You hate me for even. For the very articulating of the thought. Hate me.

RIDDLER: We are fighting for what we are.

ATTILA: Of course.

RIDDLER: The very nature of us.

ATTILA: Indeed but there might be some

RIDDLER: **Which is beyond, outside and actually indifferent to the individual death**

ATTILA: Yes, but

RIDDLER: **It also dies** (*Pause*)

ATTILA: So what if it dies. (*He lets out a cry.*)

I said it! **What if it dies so what!** I said it! I said it! (*Pause. The sound of* RIDDLER's *ruler*)

I'll make some tea, shall I? (*She ignores him. He starts to go, stops.*)

I don't look at statues, Mother. And I don't read books.

RIDDLER: I know you don't.

ATTILA: And gardens, which are the pride of this city, I couldn't give a... (*Pause*) **And anyway the gardens have been wrecked by the artillery so** (*He sobs, moans.*)

I'm sorry but...

I'm sorry...

RIDDLER: Make the tea, then.

ATTILA: Yes...

RIDDLER: Even if it's made of privet. We call it tea, don't we? **Tea we say**. A sort of memory... (*He laughs, weakly, goes out.*)

I must know who I am. I need the city to know who I am. And the city must have walls or how can I — (*Hammering on the door, violently.*)

SEEMORE: **I'm back**!

I'm back!

My love!

Scene 5

Headquarters of the army. Distant sound of violence. Cartridge paper shifts on a desk.

PLEVNA: This is very clever, but —
RIDDLER: Please don't call it clever, it diminishes it. It humiliates a person of profoundest thought to be called clever. I would go so far as to say it is a breach of manners.
PLEVNA: No offence intended.
RIDDLER: It is far beyond cleverness, which is cheap and whimsical. This is the personification of imagination and excruciating labour. I assure you. I was up until the daylight tapped me on the shoulder.
PLEVNA: Yes. It's all those things and I was wrong. What do you think?
PRAXIS: How does it move?
RIDDLER: On rails.
PRAXIS: Rails? And where are rails to be discovered? There is no timber as you perfectly well —
RIDDLER: There is timber —
PRAXIS: Perfectly well know —
RIDDLER: It is merely in the wrong place —
PRAXIS: Where is it, then? I'm sorry, do I sound annoyed? I don't intend to, but you are —
RIDDLER: Plenty of timber —
PRAXIS: So knowing all the time it grates —
RIDDLER: On what?
PRAXIS: My ignorance, perhaps. Where is this timber?
RIDDLER: Holding up the palace roof. (*Pause*)
   Two hundred lengths of oak and planed. (*Pause*)
   A system of these rails will run inside the city walls on which the
PRAXIS: **Wait** (*Pause*)
   Please wait... (*Pause. The distant sound of battle.*)
   You see, we need to keep in mind — please do not interpret this as an impertinence on our part — you certainly know this as well as me and I don't know why I feel it necessary to remind you but —
PLEVNA: The palace?
PRAXIS: What we are defending is —
PLEVNA: The palace?
PRAXIS: Our culture and our values which —
RIDDLER: All right, it'll have to be the temple. (*Pause*)
   The wheels must run on —

PRAXIS: I understand —
RIDDLER: Rails or —
PRAXIS: I understand that but —
RIDDLER: The machine cannot manoeuvre quickly and —
PRAXIS: **Of course it cannot be the temple**. (*Pause*)
RIDDLER: No. It cannot be the temple yet. (*Pause*)
>The swiftness of the machine will stagger them. As soon as they apply their rams it will appear adjacent to them and snatch their rams up with its beak, crew and all. Imagine their confusion, imagine their despair, the sad red glow under their eyeballs as they sense, as they witness, our incomparable mystery **You know it works and so do I, it is only a matter of will**. (*Pause*)
PLEVNA: Now you are shouting.
RIDDLER: Shouting? No, that's emphasis. (*Pause*)
>Furthermore, I suggest at nights we put a choir inside to irritate them with our music, which I know they hate. And move it from place to place, to kill their sleep.
PRAXIS (*wearily*): You are ceaselessly imaginative...
RIDDLER: Isn't that expected of me?
PRAXIS: Yes... Yes... I am not ungrateful... only... might these choirs not... stimulate them... rather... to a hatre which... (*Pause*)
RIDDLER: Yes...?
PRAXIS: Which... (*Pause*)
>Of course they already hate us but... (*Pause*)
RIDDLER: Forgive me, if I ask this... not to chide you but... not to provoke you even but... (*Pause*)
>Do you really want to win? (*Pause*)
>I think we must know if we really want to win... or if our efforts are... only a prelude to surrender... a decency of some kind to smother all that's abject in us... I sometimes feel... alone...
PLEVNA: You have chosen to be alone —
RIDDLER: In will. And in conviction. Solitary. (*Pause*)
PRAXIS: How arrogant you are... as if you alone possessed the virtue of the city... (*Pause*)
PLEVNA: I'll order the removal of the —
PRAXIS: Demolition is the word —
PLEVNA: Roof beams from —
PRAXIS: **Demolition is the word**. (*Pause*)
>And the rain will come, and the furniture will be —
PLEVNA: We can remove the furniture —
PRAXIS: And the murals will be —
PLEVNA: The murals, yes —
PRAXIS: Spoiled, and the mosaics —
PLEVNA: The mosaics might possibly —
PRAXIS: **How much can be sacrificed before how much**
>(*Pause*)

No, her ideas work. And that must be the sole criterion.

PLEVNA: I'll give the order, then.

PRAXIS: Give it, give it, yes... (PLEVNA *goes out*.) The city is not beautiful now, is it?

RIDDLER: No.

PRAXIS: What with their bombardments and —

RIDDLER: My inventions —

PRAXIS: Your inventions, yes, beauty certainly has deserted us...

RIDDLER: And yet we have our heads.

PRAXIS: Our heads, yes...

RIDDLER: That is the territory, is it not, that we are defending? Because of what is in our heads, when they have gone, we can rebuild again. What we are is in our heads.

PRAXIS: Yes... (*Pause*)

Now, are you quiet enough? Is it really silent there?

RIDDLER: Yes...

PRAXIS: No trouble from the poor? No trouble from the starving? They say your lamps burn all night long.

RIDDLER: Thank you, yes...

PRAXIS: You are our wall! You are our armour! (*She turns to go*.) Did you have a husband? Forgive me asking, but... I believe in manners but sometimes, we are seized by curiosity...!

RIDDLER: No husband, no. My son's the product of a single night of love. If love it is when strangers collide in chaos... (*Pause*)

PRAXIS: How I should like us to be friends. In other circumstances. How I should love to probe your life...!

RIDDLER: I should not allow it. (*Pause*)

PRAXIS: No... (*Pause*)

Some of our men attacked last night and burned their bakery! This initiative restored morale, at least until the smell of baking bread drifted to our garrison. They have not seen a loaf for months, and it played havoc with their bellies. A sound idea can have bad consequences...

RIDDLER: They should have consulted me. I could have predicted which way the wind would blow.

PRAXIS: Yes.

RIDDLER: The idea was not flawed, only the execution.

PRAXIS: Yes. (*Pause*)

They wanted to do something on their own initiative! (*She laughs. Pause*.) I'll see to it all plans are submitted to you for your comments. That would be better, wouldn't it?

RIDDLER: I think so, yes.

PRAXIS: All projects, small and large, should have your authority.

RIDDLER: Yes.

PRAXIS: Your stamp. Your imprimatur.

RIDDLER: Whatever you say —

PRAXIS: Yes, yes, it's obvious... (*Pause*)

I shall continue to live in the palace. I shall have a shelter propped against a pillar, at least... until you want the pillars... and watch the weather wash the plaster out...

Scene 6

A street in the city. A cacophony and running feet.

RIDDLER: What is this! (*A roar, a rush.*)
SENTRY: A panic, Mrs.
RIDDLER: A panic, why?
SENTRY: Who knows what makes a panic?
RIDDLER: Ask them!
SENTRY: I don't think they want to stop.
RIDDLER: **Stop running**.
SENTRY: No, that won't —
RIDDLER: **Stop running, what are you running for!**
SENTRY: Mrs, I think —
RIDDLER: **You trod on my foot!**
SENTRY: It's a river —
RIDDLER: They've made a mistake!
SENTRY: It's a river, I said —
RIDDLER: **Well, the river's made a mistake!**
SENTRY: Get into the doorway —
RIDDLER: Hey, all of you, stop!
SENTRY: I'm keeping you here, I'm doing my job and don't shift! (*They pelt past, shouting.*)
RIDDLER: Incredible spectacle... a sickness... and their eyes... are all white... they are solid... a mass without an idea... energy ignited by fear... **I do think this is a fascinating and profoundly educative**... (*Pause*) It's ecstasy...! Do you see, it's actually ecstasy!
SENTRY: Don't leave the doorway...
RIDDLER: I'm not going to leave the doorway! (*She watches, something shatters.*)
   They cannot even calculate — they do not separate — their fate from their reason — **That's ecstasy, surely?**
SENTRY: Don't ask me, Mrs...
RIDDLER: I think... in some part of my heart... in some dim corner of my thought where sunlight never strays I sought this...! (*The crowd fades past.*)
   Give me my bag now and go home. I am nearly at my house. Join your family. I am perfectly safe.
SENTRY: Whatever you say, Mrs —
RIDDLER: And wait!

SENTRY: What, Mrs?

RIDDLER: The enemy has not broken in, I assure you. We have merely yielded up the bastion. The bastion, however, is undermined. All is calculated, I promise you. Even the disasters.

SENTRY: Thank you, Mrs! (*He starts to go.*)

RIDDLER: It's a comedy! (*He stops.*)

SENTRY: Is it?

RIDDLER: A comedy, yes, I promise you... (*He goes.*) Oh, this is the pinnacle of my life, and all hereafter will be shallowness, intangible, as old women in high rooms observe the street through mirrors they once pranced in...

SEEMORE (*behind her all the time*): Don't move, I could swallow the words that fall from your mouth. Don't move. I could swim in your tempers. Move and I'll hurt you. You are in my doorway, I live here, this was once a florist's but flowers, what are they, the siege has withered flowers, and I let you in, I don't bar you, am I not hospitable, move and I'll hurt you, aren't my manners superior to yours?

RIDDLER: Don't touch me, I hate to be touched...

SEEMORE: Indeed, and I am struggling with my fingers, they are in mutiny against my orders, they want to run amok in all your garments but I am **commanding them** aren't I a ruthless man they are yearning from their sockets —

RIDDLER: **I so hate to be touched...**

SEEMORE: I can see that from your cleanliness, there is no mark of man on you —

RIDDLER: None, no...

SEEMORE: White blouses and —

RIDDLER: Cream —

SEEMORE: Cream, is it — and the fringes sewn like little gardens —

RIDDLER: It's called embroidery — listen, I am frightened of you, I confess it — **do not lay another finger on me!**

SEEMORE: The finger is so impudent God knows where it will travel, **down—inveterate—explorer!** (*He slaps himself on the hand.*)

RIDDLER: I shouldn't have sent my man away —

SEEMORE: That was an error —

RIDDLER: Yes —

SEEMORE: Uncommon error —

RIDDLER: Yes, I don't make many, I yielded sense to charity, these little kindnesses can wreck your life, **I do not like you let me go**, don't you understand you are a threat to the city if you upset my concentration it will weaken our defences **I am valuable**. (*Pause. A distant roar of masonry. As it subsides, her laughter trickles. Pause.*)

SEEMORE: What pleasure it gives me to see you smile... (*Pause*)

Immense pleasure and I love you... (*Pause*)

RIDDLER: Very well. Love me. Now let me go.

SEEMORE: When I was young I courted, how I courted, flowers, letters and so on, but that's old decorum, here's a picture of me as a youth —

RIDDLER: I am really not interested in —

SEEMORE: There! What cleanliness! I was afraid to speak to women! I blushed to look at a knee.

RIDDLER: You have matured quite remarkably —

SEEMORE: And my skin! Whiter than yours, I promise you. (*Pause. She looks at the photograph.*)

RIDDLER: Yes. Your mother must have loved you very —

SEEMORE: Adored me and ironed my shirts so stiff it slit my throat to wear them... (*She laughs. Pause.*)
All's changed and the best are gone **why are you talking friendly** do you think I'm lulled by it, my mother's grave's beyond the wall, I expect they've pitched their tents in it —

RIDDLER: Oh, I don't know —

SEEMORE: Yes, they desecrate our graveyards obviously —

RIDDLER: Yes, yes, they do — now let me go, I have not slept for seven nights and I've a child expecting me — (*She stops.*)

SEEMORE: A child...?

RIDDLER (*embarrassed by her mistake*): A child... well... not a child but —

SEEMORE: Kiss me. (*Pause*)

RIDDLER: My mouth's my own. (*Pause*)
Now, give me the little picture of yourself and I'll fasten it to my drawing board, I promise you. (*Pause*)
I promise! (*Pause. Suddenly he kisses her. A slight struggle.*)
That was unjust! That was unfair of you...!

SEEMORE (*departing into the street*): My first kiss.

RIDDLER: Vile man...!

SEEMORE: Will make a way for others...

RIDDLER: Vile...! (*A door slams.*)

Scene 7

RIDDLER *enters her house.*

RIDDLER (*calling*): It's all right...!

ATTILA: What's happening! What's happening!

RIDDLER: It's all right...

ATTILA: Where have you been **People ran like dogs like mules I never saw people so** —

RIDDLER: Me neither —

ATTILA: Horrible! I thought they'd burst in and do God knows what to me, I cowered in the pantry!

RIDDLER: Plenty of room in there! (*She laughs.*)

ATTILA: Not funny!

RIDDLER: No...

ATTILA: Not funny when you are still trembling —

RIDDLER: No, of course —

ATTILA: As I am!

RIDDLER: Indeed, my dear, sit down and I will take your hand and —

ATTILA: Don't want my hand taken!

RIDDLER: Very well —

ATTILA: And then this — horrible — this — shaking — of the floors and —

RIDDLER: The bastion has fallen —

ATTILA: The bastion —

RIDDLER: **By design.** (*Pause*) They filled it with their troops. And they have perished. What was alive is dust. What breathed is history. (*Pause*)

ATTILA: You like it.

RIDDLER: I —

ATTILA: You are — your eyes tell me —

RIDDLER: We must defend our —

ATTILA: **Beyond duty and all that is pleasure.** (*Pause*)

RIDDLER: Yes... Yes, I admit it, Attila... (*Pause*)

ATTILA: If you leave me alone again when everything is flinging like that I'll —

RIDDLER: Pleasure, yes, it must be pleasure... (*Pause*)

ATTILA: Why aren't we — talking — with them? And suggesting terms for —

RIDDLER: Terms for what?

ATTILA: A satisfactory conclusion of — **There is a light in your eye and a quality of youth in you which I — you are invigorated and** — really rather beautiful, I suppose, walking so much straighter and energy which flickers in your fingers, who would think there was starvation here to look at you —

RIDDLER: We are not starving —

ATTILA: No, but others are and —

RIDDLER: Pain is sometimes creative. Pain is —

ATTILA: Whose pain?

RIDDLER: **The quality of gods.** (*Pause*)

ATTILA: Whose pain? (*Pause*) I seem so critical, don't I, but you made me like it. Ask questions, you said. Be a questioner, and actually I don't much, it is not my instinct but —

RIDDLER: Gods are born in pain, not pleasure. They are the product of extremity, a manifestation of the will of peoples, Attila, which flows into their mortal bodies and inspires them,

enabling them to breathe in unfamiliar airs... (*She laughs.*) Surely...? (*Pause*)

ATTILA: There is a mark on your neck...

RIDDLER: A mark...? Is there...?

ATTILA: A horrid mark like a burn... (*Pause*)

RIDDLER (*going to a glass*): Oh, yes...

ATTILA: Please cover it. I so dislike it. Wear a scarf or —

RIDDLER: I will, you choose! Go into my bedroom and you
choose. And fetch me a clean blouse!

ATTILA: I will...

RIDDLER: The streets were

ATTILA (*off*): Horrid, I should think...

RIDDLER: Horrid, yes...

ATTILA (*in the door of her room*): This one? Or this?

RIDDLER: You choose! Dress me as if I were — a lover of yours!
As if I came to you sweetly as a girl and said... (*A sound of
conflict, distantly.*)

Invent me... please... (*Pause*)

That is what girls want, isn't it? To be invented?

ATTILA: I don't know...

RIDDLER: To be seized, and made in the shape of a dream?

ATTILA: How do I know? (*He holds out a blouse.*) I think this
one. This is best, in all respects. The collar and the cuffs **You
are thriving on this siege and I am not** so nicely stitched undo
your buttons, then...

Scene 8

The walls of the city. The plaintive cry of a WOMAN.

WOMAN: My son is dead!

PLEVNA: From here you see quite clearly what the enemy is
doing —

WOMAN: My son is dead!

PLEVNA: Or do you want a glass?

RIDDLER: My eyes are excellent —

PLEVNA: They are not entirely without initiative —

RIDDLER: No one is —

PLEVNA: They are concentrating all their forces at one point —

RIDDLER: No one is without initiative, the question is, what
quality is it? There are good and bad initiatives —

WOMAN: My son! My son!

RIDDLER: They are going to attack us at a single point, and the
rest are merely diversions which —

WOMAN: **My son**!

PLEVNA (*to a soldier*): Ask that woman to suppress her grief or mourn elsewhere —

RIDDLER: In fact, their trenches on the East are filled with dummies —

PLEVNA: Dummies? You can see that without a glass?

RIDDLER: Straw men they move with cables —

SOLDIER: Hey, Mrs —

WOMAN: **I howl my grief**!

SOLDIER: Elsewhere, then, please —

WOMAN: **I wave my grief, is it not a flag also? Is it not a banner**?

PLEVNA: I cannot concentrate with this —

SOLDIER: Come on, please —

WOMAN: **I thrust my pain into the hands of others, feel, feel**!

SECOND WOMAN: You aren't the only one who's suffered —

SOLDIER: Come on, I said —

SECOND WOMAN: You should see the lists —

WOMAN: **Let the lists cry, then**!

SECOND WOMAN: You're not the only one, I said!

WOMAN: **Shame on them who do not scream**!

PLEVNA (*to the soldier*): Just get rid of her, and quickly, please!

RIDDLER: No, let her near me —

PLEVNA: I am trying to describe the disposition of the enemy and —

RIDDLER: Let her near me. (*Pause*)

WOMAN: My son is dead and the world has ended (*Pause*)

RIDDLER: Some die. My heart would smother yours with comfort if it could. But some die. Obviously.

WOMAN: Nothing justifies his death, not even the greatest justice.

RIDDLER: I understand that feeling.

WOMAN: Comfort me, then! (*Pause*)

RIDDLER: Me?

WOMAN: Yes. Aren't you the genius? (*Pause. She laughs.*) I got such pleasure once, from common things. From shopping. From cups and saucers. And now. I'm skinned. The sky itself is grit in my mouth. (*Pause*)

RIDDLER: Go on...

WOMAN: There is no breath in my lungs. And my veins are empty. (*Pause*)

RIDDLER: Go on...

WOMAN: **Absence**
Everything is absence and (*She stops.*)
What do you want to know for? (*Pause*)

RIDDLER: I've no comfort. The words have run from my mouth like a crowd flees from an army...

WOMAN: If you've a son, then —

RIDDLER: I have no children. (*Pause*)

WOMAN: How lucky you are. He was a perfect child and gave me such pleasure. **That was heaven and I never knew it**.

RIDDLER: Heaven's what we were. No more, nor less. (*Pause. Then to the soldier*.) Take her away, please, and give her what —

WOMAN: **Revenge** (*Pause*)

RIDDLER: That helps, does it...?

WOMAN: Yes. That will be a drain for all my anger...

RIDDLER: We shall kill many. That's a promise. (*Pause. She turns to* PLEVNA.) What is that to the north, have they built a tower?

PLEVNA: My concern is this, that we cannot withstand prolonged attacks upon a single point now, such is the decimation of the garrison.

RIDDLER: We must let them in, then. (*Pause*)

PLEVNA: Let them in...

RIDDLER: What cannot be resisted has to be permitted. The city must be soft like lungs, like liver, it must yield and not be bone, for bone shatters, it must swallow...

PLEVNA: Swallow?

PRAXIS: May I enter? May I listen? The army wants to break out which I said was silly.

RIDDLER: It is silly.

PLEVNA: Swallow, she says. The enemy is preparing an assault and she says swallow.

PRAXIS: Good. I dread the day she has no metaphor. I dread the silence. We will be finished. (*To* RIDDLER.) Are you getting enough rations? (*To* PLEVNA.) Pamper her. If there is one luxury remaining, see she gets it. How swallow? You mean let them in, don't you?

RIDDLER: Yes.

PRAXIS: You see, I am learning her methods. Which is a bad sign, because if I can, so can they. They study you like swotting students.

RIDDLER: They are paralyzed by suspicion. Everything appears a trick to them. Even the obvious appears false, which is a dilemma there is no escape from. So as they advance, the gates are opened. (*Pause*)

PLEVNA: They won't come in.

RIDDLER: They'll hesitate.

PLEVNA: They will sense a stratagem.

RIDDLER: It is a stratagem but they will think it is an act of treason. They will think the citizens have betrayed the city to them.

PLEVNA: Why will they? (*Pause*)

RIDDLER: Because moments before the temple will be exploded (*Pause*)

PRAXIS (*coolly it appears*): What a pity. (*Pause*) What a pity, at the very moment of your apotheosis, you exhibit the clearest evidence of an insanity. A terrible pity and not at all unknown

among the class of genius. I am grateful for all you have con-
tributed to the defence of this city, your memory will be dear to
all posterity —

RIDDLER: The temple, in exploding —

PRAXIS: A statue will be raised to you I have not the least
doubt —

RIDDLER: In exploding will be incontrovertible evidence the
city's fallen to its enemies and —

PRAXIS: **It will have. It will have fallen to its enemies and the
enemy is you.** (*A pause. A wind blows over the walls. A shout
of sentries, routinely.*) The temple is precisely what we are. The
sole point of our consciousness and the focus of their hatred.

RIDDLER: Precisely, yes.

PRAXIS: I yielded the palace, and the streets, the gardens, and
the institutes of science to your imagination, the poor hovels and
the mansions, and what is left?

RIDDLER: The temple.

PRAXIS: They are barbarians. But you are barbarian, too. (*Pause*)

RIDDLER: We lure them in. And then with channels of fire for
which I have prepared the drawings, we cut them off. Only the
fall of the temple will persuade them it is safe to enter. They
will no more credit it to be deliberate than can you... (*Pause*)

PRAXIS: You make my heart go so slowly it could stop...

RIDDLER: Yes...

PRAXIS: I'm tired.

RIDDLER: Aren't we all?

PRAXIS: **Not you**. (*Pause*)
Come with me.

PLEVNA: There's not a lot of time if this is to —

PRAXIS (*leaving*): Come with me!

Scene 9

*Interior of the temple of the city. The echoing tones of footsteps
and prayer.*

PRAXIS: Look, they drag their misery here, their grief they
spread on the mosaics, and from the sculpture they extract a
nourishment. All that is great in us is here and do not use a word
like beauty, it is a poor word for this bottomless significance. I
am the queen of this city and I will lie like all our masters
underneath the floor. We are all here and even the meanest
digger of the fields or miner worked to its creation, he or she of
every village made it if not by art, then labour. Just as the people
birth the genius, so genius rebirths the nation, and children led

dimly, blindly and imperfectly through here begin to grasp their character, do I go on, do I exaggerate? So be it. It articulates what ignorance cannot express! (*Pause*)

RIDDLER: Yes. It moves me also.

PRAXIS: Does it? Does it, Madam? This also is manners! This also is civility! Look at it! Every artist here had the whole people move his hand no matter if he felt he was a rebel!

RIDDLER: I am not without a soul.

PRAXIS: No? Look!

RIDDLER: I am looking —

PRAXIS: This is what our soldiers carry in their hearts and on their badges!

RIDDLER: I know. And every stone will be rebuilt again. And every tile hung in the same position. (PRAXIS *laughs*.)

PRAXIS: Not the same tile, however... (*Pause*)

RIDDLER: We must win. Half their army will die inside our walls and they will never again disturb us.

PRAXIS: Us? And who will 'us' be, then?

PLEVNA: It's death to lose this battle. They will cut the throats of everyone.

PRAXIS: There are deaths and deaths... (*Pause*) No, you're right, it is the price of such a stratagem. But it will wreck our people in their deepest cavities, I mean the cavities of identity. I wish I had never asked you to assist us but we had been beaten swift and massacred. History puts some peoples to sleep and others, by making them masterful, spoils them. We cannot ever be the same, win or lose, can we?

RIDDLER: No. Never the same.

PRAXIS: God, you are hard-hearted, and by that I do not mean unkind, not bereft of pity, I think you have more of that than you dare admit to, but ready always for the impossible. What are you afraid of that makes you strong like this? You see, I enjoy a paradox... (*Pause*)

RIDDLER: I don't know... I...

PRAXIS: Am I being impertinent? Today I feel impertinent. Today I feel bad-mannered.

RIDDLER: I —

PRAXIS: **Your privacy conceals** (*Pause*) Precisely what? (*Pause*)

RIDDLER: I sometimes feel... I am... a god...

PRAXIS: Yes.

RIDDLER: And gods are fearful. I made myself one.

PRAXIS: A god? How?

RIDDLER: From all the broken pieces that I was. All things in myself I was taught to revile, I turned into the tools of my own deity... but fear especially... **Fear runs through my self like blood, it swims my veins but quicker, quicker than blood and I am glad of it**. (*She laughs*.) Yes, I like my fear, but it is so demanding and I shan't live long... (*The temple door slams. A wild cry.*)

SEEMORE: **I'm unforgivable!** (*Hissing*)
Unforgivable I am!

PLEVNA: There's a madman in here

PRAXIS: It's common. The mad adore the temple. But blow it up if you must, I can't defy you.

RIDDLER: It is the price of victory

SEEMORE: **Unforgivable!**

PRAXIS: You have all the answers and I am simple. Simple, and I don't want to live into another era.

SEEMORE (*distantly*): **She's here, I know, the atmosphere contains her**! (*People hiss him.*) All right, all right, I am disturbing your contemplation but I am **roped to a love**...!

PRAXIS: Make the necessary plans, and I will sign the order.

SEEMORE: **She's here! And war is the fallacy that smothers love**. (*He comes near them.*) Isn't it? But I refuse to close my heart. **Open the gates of the heart and suffer all the consequences**. Where have you been?

PLEVNA: The madman seems to know you.

RIDDLER: I don't know him.

PLEVNA: I'll have him arrested and beaten.

RIDDLER: Beaten for what?

PLEVNA: For nothing.

RIDDLER: As you wish. And now we must begin at once to dig the fire ditches.

SEEMORE: **Don't go**.

RIDDLER: The plans are with the engineers.

PLEVNA: Already?

SEEMORE: **Don't go you are under an obligation**. (*Hissing.*)
She is! She captured me and therefore I am entitled to my ration! (*They leave the temple.*)

Scene 10

Outside the temple.

RIDDLER: The ditches must be concealed under boards or rushes. only when it is certain sufficient of their soldiers have entered by the gate should it be ignited, neither premature nor late. And when the flames rush up, slam the gates again. For this I recommend two hundred soldiers and the rest to — (*She hesitates.*)
I was looking for a word to wrap unkindness in — but no — the word is — massacre — (*Pause*)
Massacre the intruders. (*Pause*)
I said it. And when you say it. It has less —

Scene 11

RIDDLER's *house*.

RIDDLER: Massacre... (*Pause*) What are you doing? (*The sound of plans shifting very slightly.*)
ATTILA: I felt the need to know...
RIDDLER: Know what?
ATTILA: The methods of your mind, Mother...
RIDDLER: Why? Shouldn't my mind be a little strange to you?
ATTILA: It is, Mother...
RIDDLER: A little garden with walls higher than curiosity...?
ATTILA: If you say so, I am sorry, I —
RIDDLER: No — no — it's me that needs to give an explanation. (*Pause*) For some reason, even for you to come near to my work is — like a trespass.
ATTILA: That's silly!
RIDDLER: Isn't it, but — some things I cannot share — and feel bruised even by your familiarity...
ATTILA: It was — I had a longing to —
RIDDLER (*seizing him in her arms*): Yes! Yes!
ATTILA: Know your —
RIDDLER: My deepest thoughts, yes, dear one! You did!
ATTILA: You show them after all, to others!
RIDDLER: That's right, I do! To common engineers and artillerists, I do! Why, therefore, should I — (*Pause*) I can't explain it... perhaps I need to over-awe you, perhaps you alone I need to impress, and dread your discovery I am only — a draughtsman!
ATTILA: More than a draughtsman!
RIDDLER: More, yes... I cover my work from your eyes as a child guiltily conceals an obscene drawing made on the margin of his book!
ATTILA: Yes! And that must be why I want to see it! (*They both laugh.*)
RIDDLER: Tomorrow... the temple will be devastated. (*Pause*) Don't be angry. (*Pause*) I tell you now because last time you were so frightened I was ashamed at not forewarning you. (*Pause*) This devastation is — sadly necessary and — a sort of crime, I know, to forestall a greater crime, believe me!
ATTILA: I don't mind.
RIDDLER: Please believe the temple can be rebuilt, all the plans are —
ATTILA: I couldn't care about the temple. I've never been in it. (*Pause*)

RIDDLER: Have you not? Didn't I take you as a child to —
ATTILA: Nope —
RIDDLER: An exhibition of —
ATTILA: If you did, I've forgotten. (*Pause*) Thank you for telling me. Tea? (*He goes out. Pause. The sound of hurrying feet and clatter.*)

Scene 12

A street near a private park.

RIDDLER: I never watch the details. (*She walks.*)
   I never observe the outcome. (*People pass.*)
   I plan meticulously and moreover I allow for error. I include all possible contingencies and provide the necessary substitutions for failures of will. They talk of human error but the proper thinker smothers error in precaution. (*Some shouts. Some running.*)
   I go in search of silence. I go to be alone. My brain is clean as polished saucepans, scoured and hung to rest. (*The squeal of an iron gate.*)
   It is a moment of sheer purity. I do not even announce where I am to be found. (*The gate clangs.*)
   If I were found, and they clamoured for my aid, I could not help. I would be helpless as a new born baby focussing dimly on the banal object most proximate to its gaze. No, better they are obliged, by the impossibility of discovering me, to exert their own imagination, however poor... (*Pause. Silence. A bird sings. A reverberating explosion. Birds rise in flocks with a beating of wings. The echoes fade. Silence. The bird sings again.*)
SEEMORE: They thrashed me. (*Pause*)
RIDDLER: Did they?
SEEMORE: Thrashed me but so what I've been thrashed before.
RIDDLER: Yes...
SEEMORE: It's the penalty for genius.
RIDDLER: Is it?
SEEMORE: Pain.
RIDDLER: Is it?
SEEMORE: **Is it. Is it she says. You know well**. (*Pause*)
RIDDLER: This is the last garden in Platea. I have the key. The only one, I thought.
SEEMORE: There is never only one key to a lock.
RIDDLER: So it seems, and I, more than anyone, should know that. I am, after all, the mistress of alternatives. But there, in some respects even the finest minds must be conventional.

SEEMORE: Mine's not.

RIDDLER: In all departments, not conventional?

SEEMORE: In none.

RIDDLER: Is that so? In some ways your aims appear to me somewhat conventional **why is it so quiet do you know**. (*Pause. Silence.*)

SEEMORE: The temple's gone.

RIDDLER: Yes.

SEEMORE: Isn't that enough noise for you?

RIDDLER: **Shh**. (*Silence*)
No other...

SEEMORE: What do you want a noise for?

RIDDLER: **Shh**. (*Silence*)

SEEMORE: Take your clothes off, there is no one here.

RIDDLER: Ridiculous.

SEEMORE: Some of them, then.

RIDDLER: None at all. Be quiet and keep your distance.

SEEMORE: You are so agitated, lie down, you are so taut, like a cat behind a pigeon —

RIDDLER: **Something's wrong**. (*Pause*)

SEEMORE: I like you less today. But leave a garment with me, I implore you. Something warm and intimate.

RIDDLER: Of course not — (*The sound of a ripping fabric.*)
You have torn my dress you madman. (*Pause*)
Why do you like me so? What have I about me that you must own? That you can't discover elsewhere? What?
I am not kind. (*Silence*)
Oh, listen, the gates are wide open and they have not come in!

Scene 13

The remains of the palace. RIDDLER's *footsteps hurry down the aisle, which is open to the sky.*

PRAXIS (*calling down the aisle to her*): They know your methods! I'm not angry. They have your measure! I'm not wild! (RIDDLER *comes near and stops.*)
Even the most complex hieroglyph of the most disordered mind eventually is legible. And babbles of strange languages become familiar sounds **they have the key to you**. I'm not angry. I live here now as if to make amends for vandalism I myself permitted. No roof, but for my tent, I am destitute like the whole population **Good for the soul perhaps** what happened to your dress, it's half the length it was, you alone it seems have had a battle **We**

stood like fools behind the gates full of murder for an enemy who laughed at us I like you, I do like you, you have the qualities in woman I have never had and now the population is talking of surrender, they find it hard to understand why we demolished our own temple, it is hard to explain you must admit, I've said it's sabotage and I hate lying, pull your dress round or I can lend you another **what shall we do now**? (*Pause*)

PLEVNA (*to* RIDDLER): Thank you for your services.

RIDDLER: I do not understand it.

PRAXIS: Obviously, no more can we understand how you could have persuaded us. We feel like infants in the hands of criminals.

RIDDLER: **I am not a criminal**.

PRAXIS: No, but you are persuasive and our minds were chained to yours, absurdly it now seems.

RIDDLER: It was a perfect stratagem and any power I had over you I earned.

PLEVNA: All your successes are ridiculed by errors of this magnitude, without the temple we are —

PRAXIS: Shh —

PLEVNA: **Practically without our wits**.

PRAXIS: Shh — (*Pause*)
She was superb. Superb in every quarter. But her superbness was legible. We should have known. We also are guilty.

RIDDLER: I disagree on every point.

PRAXIS: Of course you do —

RIDDLER: **It was impeccable**. (*Pause*)

PRAXIS: There is someone there as great as you...

RIDDLER: Impossible. (*She laughs.*)
Well, I say impossible — I — not impossible, of course, but — (*Pause*)
Always I revised my routes to the solution. I fought my habits and broke the backs of my routines, and always I have leant on inspiration which **No scholar of my genius can read**. (*Pause*)
Believe me, I have a further scheme — (PLEVNA *laughs loudly*.)
Don't laugh at powers you cannot even imitate!

PLEVNA: Never. (*Pause*)

RIDDLER: Your smile is the smile of a triumphant banality in which the extinction of this city sits... (*Pause*)

PLEVNA: Eloquent as ever, Madam, but sometimes it is an honour to be so abused...

PRAXIS: Do you think you are the only one who loves her race? I think you do.

RIDDLER: Listen to my scheme.

PRAXIS: We dare not.

RIDDLER: We are powerful now because —

PLEVNA: Not listening —

RIDDLER: **Powerful because we seem seem so weak**. (*Pause*)

PLEVNA: Listen. Even I — devoid of imagination, ham-fisted,

incapable of inspiration, even I, mechanical and without wit —
PRAXIS: Oh, don't say that —
PLEVNA: **Predict your posture**. (*Pause*)
   That alone is proof of your decline. (*Pause*)
RIDDLER: I'll try you from another angle. If things are so bad as
   you say, what have we got to lose? (*Pause*)
PRAXIS: I think the thing I have to lose is my own dignity, and
   given that I must be knifed on these steps sooner or later, I would
   prefer to be knifed with some pride wrapped round me than
   naked with imbecility, is that comprehensible to you?
RIDDLER: Everything we shudder at, everything we cast aside is
   a resource, believe me, even shame can be employed —
PRAXIS: **What is a resource? The humiliation of** — I am angry,
   after all — **our people**?
RIDDLER: Yes. Even that can be bent into a weapon. (*Pause*)
   You see, all this — degeneration — will tempt them into their
   final error — yes — this — manifest decline — will pump them
   so full of ambition they will — **listen, listen, my mind is racing
   like a river!**
   It outstrips itself! (*Pause. She laughs.*)
   I think you must trust a god, when you have identified her... (Pause)
PRAXIS: You are, are you, a god?
RIDDLER: What do you think a god is? It is only being more
   yourself than you dared to be. **Over the fence I leapt and found
   a greater self attending me...** (*Pause*) It's no affront if you
   think me insane. One day they will understand me. One day they
   will study me in special seminars, and engrave my name along
   the temple roof, oh, how boring this name will be to children
   taught to quote me, but never mind, of such colossi are cultures
   made... (*Pause*) Support me one more time, if only from gratitude, or because your own minds are stale...

Scene 14

Sounds of distant war, desultory. Quick footsteps in a street.

SEEMORE (*following her*): I know why I love you —
RIDDLER: Excellent —
SEEMORE: Because you love yourself —
SENTRY: Make way...! (*Curses and tumbling.*)
SEEMORE: This stiffness in you is your pride, and it is adamant,
   it is a wall to run my head against! **Boom!** Brains all over the
   wall! (*He laughs.*)
SENTRY: Stand off the path...!
VOICE: Give us some breakfast!

SENTRY: Get off the path, I said...!
SEEMORE (*running to keep up*): Yesterday they rioted for the
    foetus in the Museum of Anatomy, and they boil the skeletons,
    it's a fact!
VOICE: Give us some breakfast!
SEEMORE: I tell them, live off desire, aren't I excellent?
    Imitate me! Love!
SENTRY: Get back, there! (*Intimately,* SEEMORE *closes with her.*)
SEEMORE: I wear your garment, look! Under my tatters your red
    skirt. Who's mad?
SENTRY: Away you go...!
SEEMORE (*left behind*): Who's mad!

Scene 15

RIDDLER's *house. She enters.*

RIDDLER: I know how to win. (*Pause*)
    At the lowest point, it is revealed to me. (*Pause*)
    Obviously, this low perspective was necessary to observe the
    truth. One learns on one's knees. **Attila**! One must lie low to see
    the stars. **Attila**!
ATTILA: Yes...
RIDDLER: Your pain is over. A life of plenty I see unroll beneath
    your feet...! Thank you for your patience.
ATTILA (*puzzled*): My —
RIDDLER: Patience, Yes. While I staggered from plan to plan,
    you kept your faith intact —
ATTILA: Kept my —
RIDDLER: Yes, oh, yes, how you believed in me! Kiss me! Kiss
    me, do!
ATTILA: **We are on the edge of catastrophe**...!
RIDDLER: Yes! And therefore my resources were doubled, sharp-
    ened by extremity! (*Pause*)
    No... I praise myself too much...! (*She laughs.*) It was the bald
    idiot provided me. He follows me from place to place. He even
    touches me. Believe it or not, he is quite mannerless, but today,
    unwittingly, he —
ATTILA: Your dress is ripped!
RIDDLER: That was him! (*She laughs.*) And with an idiot's devo-
    tion, he wears the thing next to his skin...
ATTILA: Horrid...
RIDDLER: Next to his skin...! (*She goes to* ATTILA, *holds him.*)
    They say there is a genius out there can plot my plots...
ATTILA: Impossible.

RIDDLER: That's what I say. And this will prove it. Under the rags of this city, Attila, we will conceal the dazzling thing. And he can be the trigger...

ATTILA: Who?

RIDDLER: The bald man. Look, I kept his picture...

ATTILA (*examining it*): He was not always bald... why do you keep it?

RIDDLER: What he was... and what he is...

ATTILA: Why do you keep it, Mother?

RIDDLER: How clean he was, and full of hope —

ATTILA: Why do —

RIDDLER: I don't know why! Perhaps because it tells me... how simple it is to do so little with your life... how simple to be... merely mortal... (*Pause*)

ATTILA: Yes... well, some of us are... merely mortal, as you say... merely happy to exist... **Merely human and altogether poor, I do detest you sometimes** —

RIDDLER: Shh —

ATTILA (*sobbing*): I do! I do! (*Pause*)

RIDDLER: I know how hard it is to sympathize with me, because I do not shake my wounds in public...

ATTILA: Wounds? What wounds? If only you had some! If only you wounded and bled! (*Suddenly*) How will you use him? (*Pause*) What's the stratagem this time?

RIDDLER: It is so lonely, being a god. No wonder we require the adoration of the mortals, but how unwillingly they yield... **I talk like this because you make me**.

ATTILA: Yes, and you believe it! (*Pause*)

RIDDLER: I do believe it, yes, I think I do, you're right, and if it's sin, so be it, it is at least a sin of colour, it is a sin of proper beauty and not some mean thing. I love myself, Attila, and only she who loves herself can love another. Kiss me, please... (He does so, smiles.)

ATTILA: The bald idiot, what of him? (*Pause*)
Tell a mere mortal... the divine plan...

Scene 16

The quarters of the generals. SEEMORE *enters.*

PLEVNA: Come in **and eat**. (*Pause. He looks around.*)
Yes, I did say **eat**. (*He enters, warily.*)
There is food. Food exists. If not for the deserving, then for the heroic.

SEEMORE: I am not heroic. I am in love.

PRAXIS: Help yourself... go on... indulge... (SEEMORE *chews*.)

SEEMORE: Thank you.

PRAXIS: Oh, that's nothing, have some more.

SEEMORE: I don't need more —

PRAXIS: Put some in your pocket —

SEEMORE: Thank you, no.

PRAXIS: Why ever not? (*Pause*)

SEEMORE: I hate to be under an obligation.

PRAXIS: Such scruples are not common to vagrants... But then, you are not a common vagrant, are you?

SEEMORE: I couldn't say, I steer clear of other vagrants... (PRAXIS *laughs*.)

PRAXIS: Anyway, enough of that! Compliments and so on! Enough of that! You are not susceptible to things like honour, are you? Or patriotism, solidarity, and so on, they mean nothing to you?

SEEMORE: Well, you're brusque —

PRAXIS: I am brusque! Aren't I, yes, the siege will end this week and everyone is for the dagger, what are you susceptible to? (*Pause*)

SEEMORE: You know who, I think.

PRAXIS: I do, yes. (*Pause*)
She's yours. (*Pause*)

SEEMORE: Not by consent... I dare say...?

PRAXIS: Consent? What's that to you? (PLEVNA *laughs*.)

SEEMORE: Not much. I'll have her anyway.

PRAXIS: I admire your conviction. There is so little of it to be found nowadays. Please, try the fruit...! (*Pause. He goes to the table*.)

SEEMORE: I've never seen a better grape, fuller, sweeter, or more tender...

PRAXIS: Odd, isn't it? One vine lives. One vine endures in the midst of. Always.

SEEMORE: Listen, I am not a fool...

PRAXIS: No. You wouldn't be here if you were.

SEEMORE: On the contrary, I was a genius, in a field not much respected, but so what, time and talent do not always fit. I am neither mad nor innocent, just dirty and the woman is the sole object of my life, I intend to have her with or without your license, **where does this vine grow, then** I know every cranny of this place, obviously I'm here for something no sane man would let himself be hooked for, **what**, by the way that whip hurt. (*Pause*)

PLEVNA: Yes. (*Pause*)
Yes, I do apologise —

SEEMORE: White hot teeth it has —

PLEVNA: Yes...

SEEMORE: To the ends of your fingers, to the ends of your toes...
PLEVNA: Yes...
SEEMORE: Shrieking liver... shrieking bowel...
PLEVNA: Yes — I —
SEEMORE: That's all right —
PLEVNA: Deeply regret any discomfort —
SEEMORE: No, no, don't apologize, we must have cruelty, mustn't we —
PLEVNA: Cruelty, is it? Yes, of course —
SEEMORE: Must have it —
PLEVNA: I suppose we must —
SEEMORE: **Desire's cruelty, do you not think**?
PLEVNA: Well, yes —
SEEMORE: Oh, yes, for fifteen minutes I forgot the woman's face, **Pain killed pain**, no, don't apologise, whip's a relief, what's this then, only a bald idiot can do? (*Pause*)
PRAXIS (*extending a letter*): Carry this into their camp. (*A long pause.*)
SEEMORE: Carry it? It's so small you could stand on the walls and throw it. (*Long pause.*)
PRAXIS: Arguably, yes. (*Pause*):
SEEMORE: Or send a pigeon with it fixed to a leg... (*Pause*)
PRAXIS: Yes... (*Pause*)
SEEMORE: Did I tell you my mind's quick?
PLEVNA: Not in so many words, but —
SEEMORE: A quick mind and —
PRAXIS: Can't tell you what's in it, no. I can tell you however, it is not what you think.
SEEMORE: What do I think?
PRAXIS: Obviously, that it contains your death sentence, which it doesn't —
PLEVNA: It doesn't, no —
SEEMORE: My death?
PRAXIS: Something of a tradition that —
SEEMORE (*disingenuously*): Never crossed my mind for a moment that —
PRAXIS: The messenger transports his own —
SEEMORE: You'd stoop to such a —
PRAXIS: Death —
SEEMORE: Commonplace manoeuvre...
PLEVNA: No, indeed, that would be utterly predictible and this siege has been characterized, if anything, by its originality... (*Pause*)
SEEMORE: Obviously, it can't be that... (*Pause*)
PRAXIS: It's our last bid, you do appreciate... it is not even desperate... it is some way —
PLEVNA: A long way —
PRAXIS: A long way beyond desperation, yes... (*Pause*)

SEEMORE: I think she loves me, I think, whatever lies in this — (*he taps it*) is complicated beyond what's commonly perceived as complication... you are, perhaps, only in the shallows of it... paddling... so to speak... in what's an ocean of hidden motive...

PRAXIS: No doubt...

SEEMORE: The layers of a woman's love are infinite... (*Pause*) I'll go, therefore.

PLEVNA: You'll go? (SEEMORE *laughs. Pause.*)

PRAXIS: May I say this? Even had we tricked you, you would not be a fool... If you lay twitching on their torturing bench, you would not be ridiculous...

SEEMORE: Not in the least. (PRAXIS *takes the letter back.*)

PRAXIS: Collect it first thing tomorrow, at the North Gate. (SEEMORE *starts to go, stops.*)

SEEMORE: She asked for me, above all other idiots, didn't she?

PLEVNA: No other would do, she said. (*He smiles.*)

SEEMORE: I think the vine lies, also. I think even the vine does not know itself. (*He goes out. Distant sounds of war and movement of people.*)

PRAXIS: It's all right, he's gone...

PLEVNA: What does he mean, the vine doesn't know itself?

PRAXIS: How do I know what he means? You can come out now, Madam!

RIDDLER (*stepping out from cover*): He says a great deal, some of it wise and some of it foolish, but who trusts the purely wise any more than the purely foolish? The unflawed... how we hate them... the consistent, how we shudder in their presence... (*Pause*) They will kill him, but only after the trick has worked, after the lock's snapped shut. They will smother him in their ill-temper... (*Pause*)

PRAXIS: It will work, will it...?

RIDDLER: But the contents of the letter are indubitably true! The greatest stratagem is that which is no stratagem at all! The letter tells which regiments are itching to defect, and their positions on the walls. But who'll believe it when they look into his eyes? He shimmers with contradiction, cunning and deceit! They'll sense a bluff and torture him, but under torture he will become — I know the man — more incomprehensible still! They'll make a fatal error and attack us in the one place we are strong, it's inevitable! (*She cannot help a laugh of pleasure. Pause.*)

PRAXIS: And are you sorry for him, at all?

RIDDLER: Sorry? Me? These occasions don't allow for considerations of —

PRAXIS: No, but —

RIDDLER: One's culture, one's whole race is —

PRAXIS: Yes, but, even so...? Some little, smothered and possibly shameful manifestation of the thing called pity might —

RIDDLER: No. (*Pause*)

PRAXIS: I am less well-mannered than I was! I even stoop to sarcasm! Me! There is a sign of how far we are gone! No water in the basins, all the men have beards, and now, sarcasm! If your stratagem succeeds, sarcasm will be illegal as a tribute to the madman, and if it fails... (*Pause*) I'll kill myself. I am not prepared to let myself be tortured. Goodbye, I take so long now, to prepare myself, even going to bed takes hours, let alone dying.

RIDDLER (*extending a hand*): It won't fail, and I will wash you myself in the evening. (*She kisses her. The distant boom of a gun. She goes to leave, kisses her again.*)

Scene 17

The streets. A rain of falling objects, tiles, broken glass. The foot-steps of RIDDLER *and her guard.*

SENTRY: Can I leave you?

RIDDLER: Yes, I'm at my door now, leave.

SENTRY: Goodbye, Miss...! (*He hesitates.*) Shake hands!

RIDDLER: Certainly, if you wish. (*He turns to go.*) I'll see you again.

SENTRY (*stops*): Really? Do you think so?

RIDDLER: Yes, I promise.

SENTRY: You are always so — so —

RIDDLER: Yes, I am, aren't I? See you again!

SENTRY (*running off*): Goodbye, Miss! (RIDDLER *inserts her key into the lock of her door. It jams.*)

RIDDLER: Wait!
I can't open the —
The key won't — (*Pause. Sound of objects slipping, as if off roofs.*)
The key won't —

ATTILA (*from a window*): Don't come in.

RIDDLER (*looking up*): Don't come in...?

ATTILA: Just don't. (*Pause*)

RIDDLER: Attila, I must come in, it is my house...

ATTILA: **Impossible now** (*Pause*)

RIDDLER: Impossible... why...? Why impossible, Attila? (*The sound of sobs from the window.*) Let me in and we'll talk, it's a little wild out here —

ATTILA: No! No! The door is sealed.

RIDDLER: Sealed? Against me? Why?

ATTILA: Run!

RIDDLER: Run where?

ATTILA: **Run I said** (*Pause. The door opens a crack.*) I cannot save you, Mother...

RIDDLER: Do I need to be saved, then?

ATTILA: **Sorry!** (*He goes to shut the door again but her foot is in it.*)

RIDDLER: **Don't shut the door**!

ATTILA: Got to!

RIDDLER: My foot... is... (*He groans.*)
My foot — (*He struggles, then abandons it. His feet rush up the stairs.*)

Scene 18

RIDDLER's *house*.

ATTILA (*as he runs*): It's all over! Everything! It's the end! The finish! The whole damned bloody thing is **Long live the new age** don't come near me don't touch me **Long live the conquerors** mother don't dare **All power to the powerful** I'll hit you...! (*He grabs a ruler, turns at bay. Pause.*)

RIDDLER: Put the ruler down.

ATTILA: No more use for it now.

RIDDLER: How do you know?

ATTILA: No more rulers! No more pens! (*He scatters her desk. Pause.*)
Do you hear them? That's the enemy. Do you hear them? That terrible noise... is the choir of victory... (*A profound pause of perception*)

RIDDLER: Attila...
My little boy...
You have betrayed the State...
How? (*Pause*)

ATTILA: I have a mind. I also, have a mind... as fine as yours... as elastic... as wiry and as supple as your own... Mother...

RIDDLER: How, though...? (*He chuckles.*)
How!

ATTILA: I rigged up a system, which I call **signing**. It's done with lenses and with lights...

RIDDLER: And I thought you went onto the roof to think...

ATTILA: I did... (*He laughs.*)
Kiss me! kiss me! I also am so clever! (*She stares.*)
It works! (*She goes to him. They struggle. A quarrel and an embrace. The sound of warfare in the street rages. At last, they cease.*)

RIDDLER: My genius... my dear one...

ATTILA: Forgive me. They promised me my life. (*She separates herself, smooths her dress.*)

RIDDLER: Well... certainly you deserve to live... you alone deserve the gift of life... for you so earnestly desire it... is that the explanation for the blue thing on the door?

ATTILA: Yes! It's a sign to all their soldiers that I am not to be destroyed... (*Pause. She admires him.*)

RIDDLER: Well, obviously, I saved your life, which was my very first intention —

ATTILA: No, forgive me, I must correct you, I saved my life.

RIDDLER: Yes, but by sheltering you, I lent you the power to betray, so —

ATTILA: Half and half! How's that? (*They grin at each other.*) You loved this crisis. You loved the pain.

RIDDLER: I was in my element. How bored I should have been in peace and reconstruction. This is altogether better than success, listen, you gave away not only this, but also —

ATTILA: The other, yes. (*Pause*)

RIDDLER: I know my stratagems were faultless...

ATTILA: Possibly. But who will ever know it now?

RIDDLER: I never failed. Not once. **I must tell them I never failed! I must announce it**.

ATTILA: Stay here, they might just —

RIDDLER: They thought I'd failed, **I never!**

ATTILA: Don't go into the streets, they're slaughtering!

RIDDLER (*hurrying out*): Live your life and flourish, **I did not fail I was ever perfect!** (*The door slams.*)

Scene 19

The streets in a massacre. A cacophony of pains and delights. She races.

RIDDLER: Hey! I was impeccable! Hey! I did not make — **one error** — even one — but — **my mind was engine-like in its perfection** — let go of me you — I — (*A ripping of cloth.*) Ha! No, don't stop me you clumsy — (*A groan.*) I'll leap you like a deer, yes! (*Desperate running.*)
I'll glide like an owl through your — (*A curse.*)
I was immaculate you clot of mortals!

Scene 20

The palace. The sound of murder is distant here. RIDDLER *walks the length of the roofless aisle.* PRAXIS *is kneeling before a basin.* RIDDLER *stops. At last* PRAXIS *looks up.*

PRAXIS: Privacy?

RIDDLER: Not any more...

PRAXIS: Or manners?

RIDDLER: None. (PRAXIS *washes her neck.*)

PRAXIS: I found some water... not of the very best condition but... water...

RIDDLER (*kneeling*): I'll wash you. (*The sound of water in a bowl. Pause.*)

PRAXIS: So it failed... but what of it...? I could not have stood your triumph, frankly, I could not have borne you to be perfect, and you are so hard in the heart... I am cutting my wrists...

RIDDLER: Yes...

PRAXIS: And give me the pillow... can you stand the sight of so much blood?

RIDDLER: I don't know yet...

PRAXIS: There is something proper in frailty which the permanently triumphant never know... I am so glad you failed, though we all perish of it, why do you turn your head away?

RIDDLER: Because —

Because I am struggling with myself...

PRAXIS: Listen...! (*Shouts off.*) The new world crashes through the old... we deserved to die —

RIDDLER: **We did not. We did not. No**. (*A gasp, as* PRAXIS *cuts.*)

PRAXIS: Shh... sweet failure... shh...

RIDDLER: Yes... a failure... me... (*She gets up, turning her back on* PRAXIS, *who dies. Footsteps are heard approaching up the roofless aisle. They stop. Distant horror blowing like a wind.*)

SEEMORE: Not dead me. (*Pause*)

Oh, your smile is so —

RIDDLER: My smile?

SEEMORE: **Not dead and you are perfect**. (*Pause*)

Don't kiss me yet though I know how hard you want to

It worked

It worked

Genius

I knew it would I gave myself into your hands for love

RIDDLER: What worked...? (*His laugh. Pause.*)

SEEMORE: All as you intended, my strategist of love. **And its complexity!** Who would not adore a woman for whom love was such a maze, who made desire into a **Labyrinth**? I alone deserve you **Don't kiss me yet I know how hard you want to.** (*Pause*) They perish in their thousands, but that's a small price for our unity... I've earned you... I have passed every test... when I reached them with the letter it was as if they were expecting me **that's how smoothly it worked my genius**

RIDDLER: **What did!** (*He laughs again.*)

SEEMORE: I think you are the most divine thing ever spewed from the fluids of this planet... what did, she says... (*He chuckles.*) The vine does not know itself... but the horticulturalist... he does... the stratagem contained its own flaw, which kept me safe for your own hunger, genius... **Love me then in any way you choose it**...! (*Pause*)

RIDDLER: It isn't true...

   What you are saying...

   Isn't true...

SEEMORE: The vine does not —

RIDDLER: **This vine does**. (*Pause. Sounds of a collapse, nearer, which concentrates her mind.*) Of course I did... of course I did... loved one... (*Pause*)

   Oh, beat me! Beat me for a liar! You know me better than I know myself! (*She throws herself into his arms.*)

SEEMORE: Flawed one...

RIDDLER: Me, yes...

SEEMORE: Imperfect one...

RIDDLER: Me, yes...

   My flesh usurped my mind... Desire played its old havoc with Reason... (*He laughs.*)

   Play me, like your instrument... (*She straightens herself.*)

   Shall we go now? Someone must escape, it could be us...

SEEMORE: Am I not the vagrant? I know this city, all its sewers and its passages...

RIDDLER: Like me! As you know the city, so you know me! (*She laughs. He throws open the lid of a sewer in the floor. It rolls to silence. He indicates the aperture.*)

SEEMORE: Down there... (*Pause*)

RIDDLER: Down there...? (*The sound of water swirling.*) It's strange, but I have such a —

SEEMORE: No other way...

RIDDLER: Reluctance to deliver myself into the hands of others... (*Pause*) Silly...

SEEMORE: Yes...

RIDDLER: Since your hands are so —

SEEMORE: It leads to the river.

RIDDLER: Loving... (*She looks down.*) **It's full of water...!**

SEEMORE: Yes... I'll give you my hand... (*He goes down first.*

She is about to follow, but returns to the body of PRAXIS *and straightens the arms, folding the hands on her chest. His hand appears from the aperture.*) My hand... (*She hesitates. The sound of approaching chaos.*) **My hand...!** (*The hand stays, waiting, chaos comes nearer.* RIDDLER *does not move.*) **My hand...!**

THE EARLY HOURS OF A REVILED MAN

CHARACTERS

SLEEN	A Novelist, A Doctor
OLD WOMAN	A Patient
JANE	A Former Mistress
CRICK	A Former Colleague
ROON	A Student
POLICEMAN	
FIRST DELINQUENT	
SECOND DELINQUENT	
APPRENTICE SURGEON	
PROPRIETOR	Of a Café
TAYLOR	A Vagrant
ENTHUSIASTS	For Religion
FIRST MAGISTRATE	
SECOND MAGISTRATE	
CARETAKER	Of a Museum
THE WOMAN	A Tenant

NB The play requires a permanent presence of the city

Scene 1

A surgery in a poor district.

SLEEN: Look, I have come out in a rash. (*Water runs into a basin.*) As if my wound were not sufficient punishment I have come out in a rash and inevitably I will trip tonight. I will go down stick slithering and jaw to the kerbstone. (*A crapulous coughing.*) I will lie like an abandoned stool in the gutter and they will think another alcoholic. Only the alcoholics will know he is not one of us, he loves consciousness too much. They will circle near like the hyena, and nipping in will take my wallet. They will take my wallet, oh. And nipping in, they will take my purse. My purse, oh. (*The wheels of a train. The shuddering of bottles.*) Don't go out, then. Or if you must, leave behind your wallet. Good advice but I ever ignored the best advice. I ever clung to my policy. What's your trouble?

OLD WOMAN: Pain in the —

SLEEN: Pain! Pain, you are always here for pain! Are you certain this is pain? Perhaps you exaggerate? Perhaps it is only discomfort?

OLD WOMAN: It's pain.

SLEEN: All right, take off your clothes.

OLD WOMAN: Take my —

SLEEN: Clothes off, yes! I am entitled to my savagery! Listen, when you are gone I shall begin my novel, so think as you articulate your problem how literature shrinks with every second your pain needlessly occupies my time. There, you are burdened with responsibility! To humanity! To posterity!

OLD WOMAN: It's time I found another doctor...

SLEEN: Yes, but who would have you? You are a permanent feature of the waiting-room. No wonder I keep you till last. (*The passage of hooligans.*) You also have a rash, or is that poverty?

OLD WOMAN: I never saw no rash.

SLEEN: Then I shan't waste time on it. What hurts? Your hernia is stable. I hope you will not harp on about your hernia.

OLD WOMAN: You should be shot. The way you treat the sick. You should be shot.

SLEEN: I should. Undoubtedly it is right I should be shot, and you see, I was shot, but not sufficiently for you, it seems. The bullet passed through seven organs. Do you want to see the wound?

OLD WOMAN: No.

SLEEN: No, you do not want to see my wound, my wound has no interest for you, you only want to show your pain, my pain, my pain, she cries, but the doctor also suffers, shh! Shh!

OLD WOMAN: You are a good doctor, Doctor Sleen.

SLEEN: I am.

OLD WOMAN: You must have your jokes.

SLEEN: I must, if jokes they are.

OLD WOMAN: No other swine will see me.

SLEEN: No other, no, and what's more I charge you nothing. I am an angel. I am a god.

OLD WOMAN: You are, so abuse away!

SLEEN: Thank you. Now are you ill or do you merely want a conversation?

OLD WOMAN: I don't know.

SLEEN (*handling her*): Does that hurt?

OLD WOMAN: No.

SLEEN: Or that?

OLD WOMAN: No.

SLEEN: The rich and poor are equally obsessed with medicine. The rich from boredom and the poor — there?

OLD WOMAN: Yes!

SLEEN: From insignificance. You think pain qualifies you in some way. You think pain gives you purchase on an indifferent universe. I suffer, therefore I am observed! I'll give you something.

OLD WOMAN: Oh, thank you, doctor!

SLEEN: It will not make a jot of difference.

OLD WOMAN: Of course not, but thank you all the same.

SLEEN (*scrawls on a pad*): There, now, I have used you as badly as you have used me, I have poured my learning and contempt on you as a drunk vomits intolerance into a listening ear, I have played the genius and master to you, I have employed you as a mirror — not a very clean mirror — to reflect my own wit and unhappiness. Pass my stick. Why should a man like me require you? But I do. Why is it?

OLD WOMAN: Get married, doctor.

SLEEN: Yes, I must. I must be smothered in some way. Lock the door on your way out. Release the catch or I shall be beaten and the drugs ripped from the cabinet.

OLD WOMAN: Good night!

SLEEN: How I love the poor!

OLD WOMAN: We know you do!

SLEEN: How I love to practise in poor districts!

OLD WOMAN: We know! And we applaud you! (*A door. An inrush of the city. The door closes.*)

SLEEN: I blame the Jew. Everything fails to be proper. This is the Jew. I was punished for saying so. Who could it be but the Jew?

Shh, I was punished for saying so. Shh! (*An effort of writing.*)
I
Scrawl
My
Anger
I
Scrawl
My
Intemperate
Abuse
I
Do
The
Unfashionable
And
Untolerated
Thing
I
The
Racist
I
The
Vile
And (*A falling chair.*)
Can't breathe! (*A falling crock.*)
Air! (*He stumbles.*)
Can't breathe!

Scene 2

He walks the city. His stick taps.

SLEEN: Some years ago I should have found a mistress. This
would have been my first recourse. (*A burst of intoxicated
laughter. A staggering of heels.*) And in her dishevelled room,
all little bottles and pulp of undistinguished poets, I should have
lain with my eyes on the ceiling rose, the conversation not
flowing, the conversation false, a cloud of compliments, etcetera, a cloud of flattery, etcetera, not lucid, nor limpid, but —
(*The grinding of heels.*) **Don't knock into me I am a war
veteran!** (*The stick continues.*) They fling you over, they topple
you, how easily toppled we are! And rightly, since we have so
presumptiously risen onto our hind legs, no wonder we topple,
of course the war was ecstasy, but who dares say so now? (*He
shouts.*)

I say it was ecstasy! (*A cry from an obscure place.*) It refused distinction. It ridiculed our struggle for variety, cutting the sensitive and the vile in equal quantities. It reduced the ugly and the beautiful to a single bloody shape. How democratic it was! There was democracy for you! That and disease! But who dares say so? The young are worse than ever. At least I thought. I did think. I did relentlessly cogitate. Does he? Does she? (*The same cry rises.*)

Listen, someone is being strangled under the bridge... (*It comes again.*)

Or is it love? (*A coarse laugh, distant.*) I cannot intervene. I cannot raise my stick in protest at an act which may be justified. How can we know? How should we act? (*A woman's laugh, distant.*)

I take out my flask. I take out my leather flask and putting my elbows on the parapet, my stick in the crook of my arm, I go — (*A gulp.*)

Oh, city! (*He gulps again.*)

Oh, we are so impossibly numerous! (*He gulps.*)

Oh, city! (*He exhales profoundly*) And we are as yet still inchoate...! God help us, still inchoate... (*The slide of damp traffic. An approach of heels. The heels stop.*)

JANE: Sleen? Is it you? Sleen? I stopped the car. I said that is the unmistakeable figure of Sleen propped against the parapet.

SLEEN: How can it be unmistakeable? It is forever changing. I am both thinner and more stooping than I was even a month ago. Or was that a compliment? You cannot speak without uttering a compliment. How can we progress if everything is compliments? You were always thus. It finished us, the complimentary nature of your love.

JANE: It is a pity you were not killed in the war, Sleen.

SLEEN: So I have always argued.

JANE: Walk with me. Have you locked the surgery?

SLEEN: Yes.

JANE: And barred the cabinet against thieves?

SLEEN: Yes.

JANE: Put your arm in mine.

SLEEN: Thank you. (*The cry rises.*)

SLEEN: There it is again.

JANE: Someone is being strangled under the bridge...

SLEEN: My own view exactly! We have not changed! We are as close as ever! What is seven years? This is the lingering effect of love, which draws two minds in one direction...

JANE: Yes, but whose...?

SLEEN: Where are you taking me? I cannot be out late. I am writing the Fifth Democracy.

JANE: The Fifth? Did the first four not bring you enough misery?

Scene 3

A reception in a vast chamber. The roar of conviviality.

CRICK: Sleen! They tell me you are nursing the poor in the criminal quarter!

SLEEN: I am, but for despicable reasons.

CRICK: And writing a book in the early hours?

SLEEN: That's true as well, and for despicable reasons.

CRICK: How good a doctor are you? Perhaps you would take a look at my wife?

JANE: He is not a good doctor at all, are you, Sleen?

SLEEN: I am not a good doctor, but perhaps he does not want his wife to be cured? It is hard to tell why husbands bring their wives to surgeries, or women their husbands. Often, it's love, but equally often, it's delight. They sit and plan their widowhood. No, I have rough hands, I lack technique and the bedside manner never did come easily, but perhaps you want her to suffer?

CRICK: You are a menace to conviviality. Pork? You are the dread of kindness. Salmon?

JANE: Shall I put you in a seat?

SLEEN: Yes, find me an alcove. (*She moves away.*) Jane! (*She returns.*) Your charity is misdirected.

JANE: Yes. You mean you feel no gratitude?

SLEEN: None at all. It is something I learned from the poor.

ROON: Mr Sleen?

SLEEN: I am Sleen, yes.

ROON: Your first book changed my life.

SLEEN: Is that so? It changed mine also.

ROON: I detest sycophancy, but —

SLEEN: No, be sycophantic, there is great satisfaction in it, the heart cries out to stoop, I know, the spirit aches to genuflect.

ROON: The question that recurs however, is whether my life was changed for the better.

SLEEN: And what is the answer?

ROON: Not at all. I feel myself corrupted.

SLEEN: You see, you are hardly sycophantic at all.

ROON: I believe it licensed thoughts better submerged. It broke things, but the wrong things. I understand from the newspapers you have retired to a criminal district. I must say I think that is eminently appropriate. I think — I think — (*He falters.*)
I had a speech and now — I think you — I have waited years to say this and — inevitably I —

SLEEN: I feel sure I can construct your meaning from the dis-
    seminated parts —
ROON: I did so — I did so — want to abuse you — and — but
    skilfully abuse you — and —
SLEEN: Yes. What is the time now? I have to walk the streets.
ROON: Let me walk with you.
SLEEN: Why? I have no response to anything you say.
ROON: You are an enemy of the people! You are an enemy of
    kindness! Let me walk with you!
JANE: Are you leaving, Sleen? I have brought you a cream topping.
SLEEN: Bring the topping.
JANE: On meringue. You love meringue!
SLEEN: The meringue too. Bring it all.

Scene 4

The streets of the city.

SLEEN: If I do not walk the streets I cannot write. Why write, you
    say, it would be better if you didn't. Better for whom? Get a
    little to one side, I detest proximity, we are so numerous we
    might at least not brush, we might at least not constantly collide.
    That should be the first discipline.
ROON: Your philosophy came from your medicine. That is very
    clear. You are the only philosopher this century to have been trained
    in anatomy. It is as though your familiarity with the inner workings
    of the body produced your infamous contempt. Shit, for example.
    That word is very common in the first book, 'Democracy'.
JANE: All his books are called 'Democracy'.
ROON: I know that very well.
JANE: So you don't say a book called 'Democracy', you say 'First
    Democracy', 'Second Democracy', and so on.
ROON: I do know that.
JANE: It shortens things.
ROON: Obviously.
JANE: I met him during 'Second Democracy' and left him after
    'Fourth'. Am I to carry this meringue, or will you eat it?
ROON: Then you are the cypher known as Anna Byford! (*Traffic
    hisses, scattering words.*)
JANE: There has been endless speculation about that.
ROON: Surely, you are —
JANE: I do not know and you know even less. What are you, a
    student? He was secretive, weren't you, Sleen? Who is this
    youth? He was secretive in the extreme. He was secretive even
    with himself.

ROON: You seem angry with him.

JANE: I am not angry. The years have stilled my anger. The years have doused me where once I flamed. Wet years. Cold years.

ROON: Forgive me, but you do seem —

JANE: **Does no one want this macaroon**? I met Sleen once in seven years and the horror is we might as well have parted the day before, so little have we diverged in manner or in speech. Horror. Life is unmalleable. Life is stiff. It fractures like a brick. Horror.

SLEEN: It is no longer clay.

JANE: So you say.

SLEEN: It is baked and no longer clay.

JANE: I am putting this marshmallow on the bollard. Let him who finds it eat it. There! It sticks! What do you take me for? A carrier? A clerk? I also have a life. Give me a handkerchief.

SLEEN: She does not change.

JANE: Never.

SLEEN: Protesting but enslaved.

JANE: Ever thus.

SLEEN: And ever.

ROON: Look! The first of the starving! He creeps. He sniffs. He hesitates!

SLEEN: He thinks it may be poisoned.

ROON: Poisoned? Why? Who should poison it?

SLEEN: The haters of the poor, of course.

JANE: He licks one finger. Is it cyanide? His eyes are desperate but his imagination keeps him back. His eyes! His fear! His eyes!

ROON: Who hates the poor?

SLEEN: Only the poor.

ROON: I'll tell him. I cannot bear to see a man so —

JANE: Too late! He eats! He wolfs! He licks the bollard!

ROON: Oh, God, he does...

SLEEN: He laps where giggling debutantes have trailed their gloves...

ROON: Stop him!

SLEEN: Why, what could he tell you?

ROON: Hey! (*Passage of traffic and laughter.*) Hey!

SLEEN: No wonder you detest my books. You are irresistably attracted to the ignorant.

ROON: Vanished! In the shadows of the arch!

SLEEN: The spectacle of the cultivated prostrate before the violent and the philistine is among the more demeaning of this century.

ROON: Perhaps. I am inclined to locate virtue in the dispossessed.

SLEEN: Abnegation and self-loathing.

ROON: Perhaps.

SLEEN: Pitiful self-contempt which masquerades as curiosity.

ROON: Perhaps.

SLEEN: The intelligentsia in the vice-like grip of a fallacy. An addiction. A narcotic.

ROON: All right, and what of your fallacies?

SLEEN: The corruption of democracy. The spineless abdication of —

ROON: **I said what about your fallacies!**

SLEEN: Mine? What fallacies are mine? (*Traffic. Laughter.*)

ROON: No, I must not lose control. If I lose control of any of my arguments he will evade just criticism. He will expose my shallowness when it is his that cries out for exposure!

SLEEN: Look, the police! The police are carrying a body from the quay! I love the police! Let us talk with the police, who never read but often write. They bring me their poetry. But I am no judge of poetry, I say! Still, they bring me their sonnets. Who is it in the canvas bag?

POLICEMAN: An infant male, Mr Sleen.

SLEEN: Oh, pity the unloved child, show me... (*The canvas is unstrung.*)

He lies like a skirt in a quarry...

Oh, pity the unloved child...

JANE: You don't know he was unloved.

SLEEN: No, I don't know...

JANE: He is dead, but not necessarily unloved...

SLEEN: Not necessarily, no.

JANE: You have sympathy for no one but the dead or animals.

SLEEN: How well you know me... how little you forget...

JANE: You flagellate the living and —

SLEEN: Oh, pity the unloved child!

JANE: And venerate the dead, it is the source of your sickness!

POLICEMAN: From the label in his clothes it is obvious he was a banker's son...

SLEEN: I admire your detection. But why not a politician's? Do they not buy their children shirts?

POLICEMAN: Intuition, Mr Sleen.

SLEEN: I'm not one to quarrel with that. Has a banker missed a child?

POLICEMAN: He entered the water forty miles upstream.

SLEEN: In the better district. Through accident or suicide?

POLICEMAN: His mother hated him. She had a lover. The lover also hated him.

SLEEN: And this you know by intuition?

POLICEMAN: If it isn't true, what difference does it make? The child's dead now. Good night! (*The slamming of van doors.*)

SLEEN: I like the police. They understand the insignificance of truth. Or rather, there is a greater truth to which they owe a secret loyalty. This is the arbitrary nature of existence which disdains selection.

ROON: This is the argument of 'Third Democracy' and it is entirely spurious!

SLEEN: Only to those who cannot come to terms with pain! Now I wish you had not been so reckless with the macaroon. We are a mile from the nearest stall by my calculation. (*The rapid tapping of the stick.*)

JANE: I recognize this place... (*Traffic and cries.*)

I have not strayed from the main thoroughfares for years but now.

ROON: Come on!

JANE: Or dared stroll in the dark but now.

ROON: Hurry! Sleen is making headway!

JANE: Oh, God! The Fountain of the Virtues!

ROON: Sleen! (*Echoes among slum tenements.*)

JANE: I thought I should never pass this place again. Not that I am old. Not that I lack curiosity but. And it is built round. It is wrecked.

ROON: Sleen!

JANE: Under this fountain he spoke 'The Catechism of Erotica'.

ROON: Impossible. It was in Prague.

JANE: No, it was here. He pretended it was Prague. He thought Prague dignified it. But it was here and I was wearing black. Oh, we are fatuous, we are sham, and I hate you...

SLEEN: We are not sham. Nothing we say endures, that's all.

JANE: We are sham, and I hate you!

SLEEN: Even her underwear was black...

ROON: That's in the book.

JANE: Oh, the velocity of moments scorched and ridiculed, I must sit.

ROON: I will fetch you some water.

SLEEN: The fountain does not work. Twice they repaired it, and twice unknown parties damaged it. They elected not to repair it thrice, and who can blame them?

ROON: Please don't weep...

SLEEN: There is a limit to the patience even of municipalities.

ROON: Can I lend you my handkerchief?

SLEEN: Let her weep.

ROON: It's filthy, but —

SLEEN: Oh, let her weep! She loves me.

JANE: **You know nothing**.

SLEEN: She loves me in another form.

JANE: **You know nothing**.

ROON: Shh! (*The trickling of water from a spout.*) The fountain works!

SLEEN: Then the authorities are showing more resilience than I gave them credit for. Drink deep. Every mouthful justifies their faith.

JANE: Oh, to be here with you. You of all people! Here of all places! As if the city weren't sufficient in its sprawl, we fetch up here.

ROON: How did he state the Catechism? Was it declaimed, or did he whisper it? Were there others present? Did he have it off by heart? And was it fluent, or staccato? Or can you not recall?

JANE: It was early evening.

SLEEN: And spontaneous.

JANE: In those days spontaneity was prized.

SLEEN: As if inspiration were sufficient by itself. That is how shallow we were.

ROON: This however, was not shallow?

SLEEN: This was not. And certainly I was seized. It is so long since I have been seized I find this seizure hard to recall.

JANE: You are seized by hatreds.

SLEEN: Hatreds, yes. I had forgotten hatreds for a minute... but this was a different fluency, this was twenty sentences of pure fascination, I do not think I took my eyes off her once or even blinked, correct me if I'm wrong, I may exaggerate, I may paint the past, we do, don't we, sprinkle elaboration for effect? But —

JANE: He looked me relentlessly —

SLEEN: Implacably —

JANE: And far from kindly in the eyes, I was eighteen —

SLEEN: And prowling for copulation —

JANE: That's true, I was, the partner was of no significance to me, oh, why did we fetch up here? (*The sound of damage and ecstasy.*)

ROON: The fountain is — (*The sound of pleasure and malice.*)

SLEEN: I take out my flask! I take out my leather flask and putting my elbows on the railing, my stick in the crook of my arm, I go — (*The sound of breakage and delight.*)

Oh, City! (SLEEN *gulps.*)

Oh, we are so impossibly numerous!

ROON: They are tearing out the pipes!

SLEEN: Persuade them otherwise.

ROON: I —

SLEEN: Intercede. Remind them of the purpose of a fountain.

ROON: I —

SLEEN: Its kindness. Its refusal to discriminate.

ROON: Yes, but they — (*Squeals of delinquency.*)

SLEEN: Hey! (*Silence*)

1ST DELINQUENT: Old geezer waves a stick!

2ND DELINQUENT: How they, the old, try to command us with their monosyllables, **Hey yourself!**

1ST DELINQUENT: Oh, his warped expression, did such twisted features ever so disfigure an ancient gob? I shrink. I cower. (*The explosion of hysterical contempt.*)

SLEEN: Filth.

2ND DELINQUENT: His vast vocabulary! How he flogs us! His indignation's pure poetry! (*A further explosion.*)

SLEEN: Scum.

1ST DELINQUENT: I am crucified with shame to hear my acts

so castigated. (*Mockery, hysteria.*)

SLEEN: Filth.

2ND DELINQUENT: And again! I think the word rings better on its second coming!

SLEEN (*relentlessly*): Scum.

1ST DELINQUENT: Were we rebuked with such originality before?

SLEEN: Filth.

ROON: Mr Sleen, I think —

2ND DELINQUENT: His mouth has jammed itself into a groove.

SLEEN: Scum.

1ST DELINQUENT: The repetition is intended to inspire with its cumulative effect —

SLEEN: Filth.

ROON: Mr Sleen —

1ST DELINQUENT: But does it?

SLEEN: Scum.

2ND DELINQUENT: I think not, rather it makes me wish to stop the orifice right up —

ROON: Mr Sleen, I beg you —

SLEEN: Filth.

ROON: Mr Sleen, I can't bear violence —

SLEEN: Get out of here. You smother memory with putrefaction.

ROON: **Don't hurt him**! (*The city. Cries. Laughter.*)

SLEEN: Oh!

ROON: **Don't wound him**! (*The grinding of trams.*)

He hated the country, it says so in the Memoir. Bird song, for example, enraged him, and hedges he regarded only as a pretext for an ambush — (*The terrible sound of a thrashing.*) This was the war. Sleen fought the war with a conventional expectation of its brevity and bravery — his peculiar accents were not forged at this time — (*Cries of pain.*) Later he was shot and received a pension for considerable disability — (*A long cry and silence. The city. The sobs of* JANE.)

SLEEN: They beat me with my own stick... I knew the stick would betray me tonight...

ROON: I'm sorry...

SLEEN: Sorry, why?

JANE: A handkerchief, quick!

SLEEN: Why sorry?

JANE: He's bleeding! A handkerchief, quick!

SLEEN: I have never rebuked the coward. The coward is perfect, the coward is —

ROON: I am not a coward, I merely —

JANE: Help him up!

SLEEN: Stick!

ROON: No, I am a coward, it's true I'm a coward and I —

SLEEN: Stick!

JANE: Take his arm!
ROON: I am humiliated, though God knows if anyone —
JANE: His arm, I said —
ROON: If anyone deserved a thrashing, it must be you —
JANE: Get up, Sleen!
ROON: No! Now I am doubly contemptible! I justify my cow-
ardice by reference to his character! I excuse myself by —
JANE: **This man is bleeding and no one cares for your apo-
logies!**
ROON: Yes, yes, give me your arm...!
JANE: There is the hospital! Sleen has been beaten in the shadow
of the hospital!
SLEEN (*horrified*): Not the hospital!
JANE: The blue lights! Look!
SLEEN: Not the hospital!
JANE: How typical of Sleen to suffer —
SLEEN: Not the hospital, I said!
JANE: In the vicinity of kindness! It is as if nature could not bear
to see such wickedness become extinct!
SLEEN: Don't move me...!
JANE: Sleen, you are bleeding profusely and it is getting on my
clothes!

Scene 5

The hospital. A clatter of instruments.

APPRENTICE SURGEON: Sit still. (*A cacophony of human cries
and yells.*) I have read all your books.
SLEEN: Is that so? (*A dropped tray. An inaudible oath.*)
APPR. SURGEON: Not only your books. (*A shoal of sliding in-
struments.*) Also, your pamphlets. (*A cackle of nurses.*) Sit still.
(*The cries.*) I brought you to the head of the queue. They grum-
bled. How they grumbled! Were their wounds not painful, too?
But I recognized you. (*A distant altercation.*) You are Sleen, the
pornographer. (*A boom of heaved furniture.*) And I am Jewish.
(*A shriek of nurses.*)
SLEEN: You are going to torture me! (*An echo in long corridors.*)
APPR. SURGEON: Three pamphlets slandering the Jews...
SLEEN: I was sufficiently punished. **Did you pick that syringe
off the floor**?
APPR. SURGEON: Three pamphlets, printed at your own ex-
pense.

SLEEN: I was rich in those days **That needle is filthy**!

APPR. SURGEON: Sit still, you will make my hand shake and the needle will go all —

SLEEN: Kill me, then! Why should I care? Kill me! As if I have not been sufficiently punished! (*A crescendo of trollies.*)

APPR. SURGEON: Do you hate life, Mr Sleen?

SLEEN: That is the opinion of the well-informed, who am I to contradict it? **You are deliberately probing my wound**.

APPR. SURGEON: Mr Sleen, my longing to punish you is diminished by the certain knowledge no pain could satisfy the need.

SLEEN: Since when did that stop anyone? **If that pain is not deliberate I don't know what** —

APPR. SURGEON: There is dirt in the wound —

SLEEN: Dirt, yes, but how much? Perhaps you find dirt where other surgeons would find me clean **That swab is not sterile**!

APPR. SURGEON: Sit still or I —

SLEEN: Kill on! Murder on! Avenge! As if I were not sufficiently punished! (*A clatter of buckets and the rush of faucets.*) Come with me.

APPR. SURGEON: Go with you? Why?

SLEEN: Because you hate me. (*The murmur of the casualty room.*)
Let the sick cure the sick. (*A cry*)
The scalded infants and the drunk who fell under the wheels... stabbed politicians and the overdosed... (*A whinnying laugh.*)
Oh, doctor, oh, beloved physician! They weep their gratitude they lick your palms, **Save my miserable bone and mucus, my idiot perceptions and my pelvic thrusts, keep me from extinction**! It's false, this doctor love. I know, I practise. (*An indistinct quarrel.*)

SLEEN: Break your oath. (*Shattering glass.*)
The ecstasy of breaking your oath...

APPR. SURGEON: I am a Jew. And I will kill you before the night is out... (*A cacophony of protesting patients.*)

Scene 6

The street. The stick taps.

APPR. SURGEON: His age, far from eliciting pity in me, fills me with loathing for years he had no right to enjoy...

JANE: Enjoy? Sleen enjoyed nothing.

APPR. SURGEON: His wit, far from deflecting my contempt, fills me with disgust at his survival...

62 *Howard Barker*

ROON: It's not wit, it's terror.
SLEEN: They know! They know everything!
APPR. SURGEON: I regard the torturer as innocence itself against the pamphlet writer. Who's worse? For the act could never be committed if the thought were not articulated first! (*A door bell dances.*)

Scene 7

A café, empty.

PROPRIETOR: Mr Sleen, I thought perhaps you'd died.
SLEEN: I understand that. I am never late. When an old man is late for the first time, you think he's died. That's natural. As it happens I am merely beaten, which is nothing like dying. Or is it? How can we tell? I am here with three mortal enemies.
PROPRIETOR: Nothing new in that. When did you ever have a friend? (*Glasses, chairs.*)
SLEEN: These three ache for my extinction which is in any case imminent. But still they ache. Where is Dogg tonight? His legless trunk is stacked against the doorway. Every night he greets me as a stranger. He describes how he came to lose his limbs. Every night the description is different. Where is Dogg tonight?
PROPRIETOR: He never came.
SLEEN: The city is in profound disorder. And I have lured this surgeon from her duties, this student from his studies, and this woman from her memoirs.
JANE: What memoirs?
SLEEN **Don't pretend you are not writing your memoirs**: (*A passage of hooligans.*) We lie, don't we, even at the rim of the grave?
APPR. SURGEON: I will pay for my own brandy.
PROPRIETOR: Mr Sleen runs an account.
APPR. SURGEON: I will pay notwithstanding.
ROON: Me, too.
SLEEN: No one takes from me. I am too vile. They fear contamination.
APPR. SURGEON: Yes! Six million mouths cry out don't take from him!
SLEEN: She's right. I hear them. (*A coin rings on the table.*)
PROPRIETOR: I also was a bad man. That is why I stay open late. The bad are kind to the bad.
APPR. SURGEON: That is a contradiction. The good can be good to the good, but the bad must be bad to the bad, or you are inconsistent.

PROPRIETOR: I am not consistent, am I, Mr Sleen? Either that or I do not believe I'm bad at all, however bad the things I did. But perhaps they weren't bad, either? I rely on Mr Sleen.

SLEEN: He tortured. Day and night. He slept such sleeps in a dirty room above the station and the sun streamed in on him, washing his eyelids, and the pigeons mildly woke him, cooing on the sill, as if he were merely a printer sleeping off his shift...

APPR. SURGEON: I can't drink the drink...

SLEEN: No, of course, you would rather die of thirst.

APPR. SURGEON: Yes!

SLEEN: Back to the Casualty Ward! There life is simple! Much sewing! Much bandaging!

APPR. SURGEON: **You unkilled! You unmurdered**! No, I must be calm, I must be temperate...

JANE: How beautiful you are in your just rages...

APPR. SURGEON: I must be cool, I must be level...

JANE: Your neck is bathed in colour like a sunset...

APPR. SURGEON: Shh! Please!

JANE: Sleen, I think, whilst suffering inordinately from hate, knew very little of a healthy anger. Did you, Sleen? Know anger?

ROON: Mr Sleen submerged his anger in a sense of the absurd. I believe that to be the source of his corruption.

SLEEN: How true that is. Even the Battle of Tattlingen struck me forcibly as absurd. And I was only seventeen.

ROON: You see! Even at that age! Please go on.

SLEEN: All around me, others experienced anger. As the bombs came down. As the horses flew into the air. They felt their lives were wasted. Wasted from what, however? I would say to them, as we suffered in our holes, from what excellence are you now debarred? The dance hall? The library? What? Then the bullet entered me, ploughing through my system, at such an angle it contrived to mangle not only one, but seven organs. Seven organs! As I fell I heard them laugh, a peculiar and delighted laugh. This detachment of mine puzzled them and made them cruel. They were angry at my lack of anger.

ROON: Naturally! Your complicity with fate is among the most infuriating aspects of your work. This is what I wish to remonstrate about!

APPR. SURGEON: And yet he slandered the Jews...

ROON: This is something everybody knows...

APPR. SURGEON: If he felt no anger at anything that befell him, if he was reconciled to every blow that fate dispensed, its arbitrariness, its lack of discrimination, if this delighted him, why persecute the Jews?

JANE: Your neck...

APPR. SURGEON: If he declined to issue judgements, why did he go to such lengths to publish slanders of the Jews?

JANE: Your neck —

APPR. SURGEON: Is red! I know it is! **Do not dare to fill my glass**!

PROPRIETOR: Forgive me, it is a barman's instinct...

SLEEN: The surgeon will die if she refuses all nourishment that swine might have participated in the preparation of... (*A sound of stacked chairs.*)

JANE: So many people have the right to murder Sleen. Even I, who placed my entire innocence at his disposal, who emptied the cupboard of my personality and laid the entire contents at his feet, I also have the right to murder Sleen!

SLEEN: The proprietor is stacking his chairs...

APPR. SURGEON: Obviously, yes...

JANE: I also was slandered! I also was abused!

SLEEN: Our conversation irritates him. He only likes to hear about himself.

APPR. SURGEON (*to* JANE): Please, you are hurting my hand...

SLEEN: It is the flaw of torturers, their vanity... their inordinate vanity...

ROON: Look at his use of the word democracy. All his books are called 'Democracy'. Yet he detests mankind. For him the word democracy is synonymous with mob, crowd, riot...

Scene 8

The clatter of the doorbell. The stick on the pavement.

JANE: I was a house... or perhaps a palace... yes... why not a palace? I was a palace, into which he walked like a proprietor, and having removed the furniture, attacked the plaster, and removing the plaster, tore out the laths, and shaking the joists with his bare hands, loosened the tiles which fell like an avalanche, look out, the tiles! I was demolished, I was vandalised!

ROON: All this with your consent, however? It must be admitted, surely, this was with your consent?

JANE: I have been squeezing your hand! Forgive me, I have been squeezing your hand!

APPR. SURGEON: It's all right...

JANE: Is it? Is it all right?

APPR. SURGEON: Yes...

JANE: Good... Oh, good... (*The distant bawling of a crowd.*)

ROON: Sleen's ideas were never consistent, but it's obvious from even the most superficial reading of the books, he exaggerated their inconsistency for effect... (*The bawling is mounting.*)

SLEEN: Press into this doorway. This is the river of the young.

ROON: Someone is already cringing here.

SLEEN: Oblige him to move over. I have been hurt tonight already! (*A scraping of boots, knees, elbows.*)

TAYLOR: Oi!

SLEEN: Oi, yes! And I should be at my novel! Oi, indeed! Who are these? In all my nights I've not seen these!

TAYLOR: Coming out from Bible study...

ROON: Bible study?

TAYLOR: You think a mob can't be spewed out of a church? (*A volume of chanting and boots.*) They are going to battle with those who say the Virgin was no virgin. They clasp their books, and some of these have brass edges. These edges they bring down sharply on the noses of those who say the Virgin was no virgin.

SLEEN: Shouldn't you be at the hospital? The casualties will swamp the corridors.

APPR. SURGEON: You are always telling me my duty. The dutiful become the victims of the idle! No, I am here to learn, and having learned, to punish!

SLEEN: I deserve everything I get, but so do you. (*A shattering of glass and collision of bodies.*)

ENTHUSIASTS: Oi! Cringers!

SLEEN: Forgive us, yes, I had a headache and sank into the doorway...

ENTHUSIASTS: **Cringers, Oi!**

1ST ENTHUSIAST: Your view of the Immaculate Conception!

SLEEN: Well, it's as you say...

1ST ENTHUSIAST: How do I say?

SLEEN: The precise order of words escapes me, but I —

2ND ENTHUSIAST: Book him! Book him in the face! (*A surge in the confined space.*)

APPR. SURGEON: Stand back or I will wound you with this scalpel!

ENTHUSIASTS: A surgeon!

APPR. SURGEON: Yes, and I know every duct and culvert of your system. I will end, or ruin, or make you hate your life from a single incision. (*Pause. Boots tramping.*)

1ST ENTHUSIAST: We know him, rolled into a corner like a louse. It's Sleen.

APPR. SURGEON: You know Sleen? In this light?

2ND ENTHUSIAST: We burn his books. But some can always be discovered.

SLEEN: It is the curse of printing...

1ST ENTHUSIAST: We go into the bookshops with our lists. We turf out books which threaten the Immaculate Conception. And his mug's on all the covers.

SLEEN: No man paid a greater price for vanity. And I never

mentioned the Immaculate Conception.

1ST ENTHUSIAST: Not in so many words...

SLEEN: In no words at all —

2ND ENTHUSIAST: Book him! Book him in the eyes!

APPR. SURGEON: Scalpel! (*A pause of threat and fear. The continuing passage of boots.*)

TAYLOR: How quiet it is in the lull before a murder. Time stands still. Oh, the hiatus! Give us a sandwich, somebody. The birds are singing. Oh, the suspense! Sardine, preferably...

2ND ENTHUSIAST: It would please us to die in such a cause. But there are worse enemies than Sleen, who's senile, anyone can see. There are some enemies still stirring in their cots...

SLEEN: Yes! Seek them, before they gurgle heresy! (*The enthusiasts withdraw, shouting a slogan. Their boots hasten after the departing. A silence.*)

I can't get up.

Did anybody hear?

I fell awkwardly.

Is anybody interested?

A mule in a ditch.

A cat in a net.

I said did anybody —

TAYLOR: I read Sleen...

SLEEN: Oh, God...

TAYLOR: I read Sleen, and my life was filled with worthless hatreds...

ROON: Is that so?

TAYLOR: It is. I ascribe to him and his influence my wretched vagrancy.

ROON: It's true! Go on!

TAYLOR: I felt as if my life was balanced, like the pans of scales ...

ROON: Yes...!

SLEEN: You're encouraging him in his —

ROON: Shh!

TAYLOR: And reading him, a weight fell into one, which lurched violently, as if a girder had been dropped into it and only flour was contained within the other. And the light scale flew away, into infinity. I sank. I rotted. I abandoned hope. Did anybody find a sandwich?

ROON: This is the effect! I know! Show him your face! This is the evidence!

SLEEN: What's wrong with his face? His face is Roman, late Roman, glazed in eczema, but am I responsible?

TAYLOR: I would have been somebody!

SLEEN: They all say that, the vagrants. It's their shovel. With this shovel they scrape their graves.

TAYLOR (*lurching towards* SLEEN): My spoiled life!

APPR. SURGEON: Get off him! (*Sounds of a struggle.*)

SLEEN: How hard she fights! She will kill me and nobody else!

TAYLOR: I could have been so splendid! I could have been so fine!

ROON: Yes... yes...

SLEEN: Am I too late for the underground? Put me on a train, I have so much to write. As if I were not sufficiently accused! No, I ache to indict myself! Was there ever a man who so condemned himself? It's on every shelf! My death sentence! Am I too late for the tube? I have to write!

APPR. SURGEON: You are too late for everything. Even pity.

SLEEN: I like this woman. She never talks of the future. Only the past.

APPR. SURGEON: The past was someone's future!

SLEEN: Punish! Punish! Do you think I am afraid? I expected to die in squalor. I expected to die in a ward. I, who so detest the convivial and the smell of flesh, I expected to die in chatter and the concert of spilled pans, give me a field, I said —

JANE: He did! He did say that!

SLEEN: A silent field in winter, and let me slip between the furrows, down in the clay, down in the chalk where the dead of the last eight wars would welcome me, oh, it's Sleen, they'd say, better late than never!

JANE: Except they wouldn't —

SLEEN: They wouldn't, no —

JANE: They would accuse —

SLEEN: She knows! **Accusation is the music of my life**. And my mother was as bad, put her on trial, why don't you? We were a pack of trouble makers, dig up the dead Sleens, I will indicate the graves, I will identify the cemeteries, off with their heads and a limb on every gate! No, I hoped for a plague, I hoped for epidemics, that I might wander in a fever through frosty and abandoned villages, but I am so medieval, I am so nostalgic for the great diseases, am I going on? Do I irritate you? Anyone would think I did not want to die and was talking to save my life! The contrary, I promise you... (*A pause. Detritus blows along the gutters.*)
      What is that smell? I know that smell...

TAYLOR: It comes out of the grating. Out of the grating comes a warm wind which is worth four overcoats.

SLEEN: But the odour...

TAYLOR: It's breath. We are above the lawcourts.

SLEEN: I knew! And the music? Do they sentence to Mozart now?

TAYLOR: How would I know? I know nothing! I might have been so fine and I know nothing! This is you and your —

ROON: Shh! Shh!

TAYLOR: What might I not have been but for —

ROON: We understand! We understand! (TAYLOR *sobs. The*

music is faint, among the draught.)

SLEEN: I was everything vile. How fortunate tonight is my adieu.
   How sweet the world will be by the morning! How ordered!
   How fragrant! How compatible!

APPR. SURGEON: You are wicked. I use the word with infinte
   care. You are wicked because you make the very idea of justice
   — the very pursuit of it — (*A pause. A slap.*) I had to do that.

SLEEN: No. Smack away. I do infuriate my enemies — (*A second
   slap.*)

JANE: **Stop that**.

ROON: Yes, I don't think it helps to —

APPR. SURGEON: Oh, it does! It does help! Yes!

SLEEN: Would you mind if I — a certain weakness of the bladder
   — common to old men — and I am rarely out this late — I am
   the last man who hesitates to urinate in the gutter, some touching
   relic of civility, I have to use the cubicle, forgive me, I — (*A
   further slap.*)

JANE: Oh, you, listen, you —

APPR. SURGEON: He claims everything! And he is vile!

Scene 9

Faucets, taps, cisterns. The stick taps on tiles.

SLEEN: Why follow me in here? I can't escape, they bar the win-
   dows. This is presumably to deter the urine thieves. (*He pisses.*)
   And the music! It is a sign of our decline that we must piss to
   Mozart.

ROON: It is not Mozart, as you know very well...! Why do you
   tell lies? Why do you exaggerate? You are an eloquent husk and
   it infuriates to think how great you might have been! (*A torrent
   of water.*)

SLEEN: What do you want me to do, weep? I can weep. I have
   all the tricks of the underclass. (*A sound of coarse singing.*)

ROON: Underclass? For ten years you were rich!

SLEEN: Listen, judges! The unmistakable harmonies of judges!
   Now we are for it. This is all the consequence of pissing in
   cubicles. My quaint ethics! Now we are for it! (*A crash of a
   wooden door.*)

1ST MAGISTRATE: Oh, Sleen...! Not dead, and in our cubicles!

2ND MAGISTRATE: Sleen! Are you authorized to slash in here?

SLEEN: I tremble to think I may have offended. It said nothing
   on the door about scum of the earth.

1ST MAGISTRATE: And with a youth!

SLEEN: He follows me everywhere...

2ND MAGISTRATE: Sleen, it must be time to slap more charges on you.

SLEEN: More? Then what became of the amnesty?

2ND MAGISTRATE: It grieves so many that you are permitted to walk the streets, and looking guiltless.

SLEEN: Looking, yes, but feeling...! Should I close your door, the draughts in here are —

1ST MAGISTRATE: Sleen...

SLEEN: Yes...?

1ST MAGISTRATE: We tried to rid the world of you. We asked for death.

SLEEN: How could I forget it?

1ST MAGISTRATE: And here you are. When others hanged. When others swallowed poison.

SLEEN: Yes. But fading. And repentant. (*A rush of water. A door bangs. The stick taps on the tiles.*)

1ST MAGISTRATE: Sleen! (*The stick ceases.*) I have a battered copy of the 'First Democracy'.

SLEEN: Oh, really?

1ST MAGISTRATE: And with hand-written corrections.

SLEEN: In whose hand are the corrections? Everyone wanted to correct me.

1ST MAGISTRATE: Yours.

SLEEN: Are you sure?

1ST MAGISTRATE: I know your hand. I compiled so much of the evidence against you.

SLEEN: You did. You were young, then, and even more idealistic. (*The stick taps.*)

1ST MAGISTRATE: Have you any idea of its value?

SLEEN: Its value? Value to whom? If what it says is true, God knows its value. Shouldn't you incinerate it?

1ST MAGISTRATE: You don't change.

SLEEN: No?

1ST MAGISTRATE: For all your recantations. For all your gro-velling apologies.

SLEEN: It was never enough to confess. Nor even enough to be punished. **And I was shot through seven organs**. Never mind! Never mind! How tedious I am, drawing your attention to my pain! I cannot see a judge without exhibiting my suffering! As if that could buy you off. And I pleaded to crimes I had not committed... there is a man near the fishmarket buys my work, but he may be an agent of purification. He may buy it only to burn. I have come across such dedication before.

2ND MAGISTRATE: You are loathesome, Sleen.

SLEEN: Yes.

2ND MAGISTRATE: Though I see you pitiful as you are, old and near to a death I campaigned for, I feel nothing in your presence but disgust...

SLEEN: The vilest murderer would shine beside me in celestial
   light —
2ND MAGISTRATE: **Don't be sarcastic I loathe it** —
1ST MAGISTRATE: Michael —
2ND MAGISTRATE: **He has no shame**. (*Pause. The whispering
   of plumbing.*) Does he?
ROON: He has this terrible effect on people. But if he had been
   executed, I think he might have acquired an even greater repu-
   tation, which his silence would only magnify. Whereas living,
   his absurdity is obvious to all...
SLEEN: The verdict of youth... (*The torrent of the cisterns.*)

Scene 10

The street.

APPR. SURGEON: Where have you been!
ROON: We were accosted by the magistrates.
APPR. SURGEON: Since when did magistrates sit at night?
SLEEN: Why not? You cut at night. You sew at night. Crime
   prefers the night, so why not justice?
APPR. SURGEON: I don't trust any of you. You pretend to hold
   Sleen in contempt but he dominates you.
ROON: He does not dominate me, I detest his views.
APPR. SURGEON: Yes, and that is how he dominates you!
JANE: I know this place...
APPR. SURGEON: He wrings pity out of you even while you
   claim you wish him dead. He plays pity like an instrument.
ROON: I am not persuaded by his methods —
APPR. SURGEON: You grovel in the midst of your rebukes —
ROON: I am not for a single moment oblivious to his —
TAYLOR: You are! Any fool can see you are!
ROON: I deny it!
TAYLOR: If Sleen falls down it's always you who picks him up.
   (*Pause*)
ROON: Is that so? I hadn't noticed...
TAYLOR: You see!
ROON: It may be so —
TAYLOR: You see —
ROON: What if it is so! I still hate him!
TAYLOR: Bah!
ROON: I hate him more than you!
JANE: I know this place... this is the barracks... (*A wind in empty
   corridors.*)

TAYLOR: Was the barracks... was...

JANE: I stood against this gate, this same iron gate, pressing my breasts against the bars to a catch a glimpse of Sleen up in a window or drilling in the yard, all of us did, the intellectuals and the workers, the women in clogs, the women in leather, the high heels and the low heels, all of us man-mad and wild with wanting, we talked of them as if they were our children, and some of us were elegant, and some of us had bruises, and as they passed we stroked their hair, the blonde hair and the black, tearing off their caps and crying out how thin you are, how coarse your cloth is, the rich women and the poor, our buttocks glued together as we poured our thin arms through the railings, this same gate, this same eagle... how we loathed that eagle, but it was well-cast and no one had a hammer...

ROON: From here Sleen marched out to be shot through seven organs. When I discovered this I pitied him. I refused myself the liberty to criticize. But later I found that some who also had been shot through seven organs overcame their hate. They made of their pain a passionate plea for love. Pain is a plastic thing, and you mould it as you may.

TAYLOR: What do you know about pain?

ROON: Not a lot, but —

TAYLOR: **What does he know about pain**?

ROON: You see, I can't say anything... always, I sound false...

TAYLOR: Always...

ROON: I was thinking of Schleiss — (*The tapping stick stops.*)

SLEEN: Schleiss was not shot in seven organs!

ROON: No, but —

SLEEN: Schleiss was a pilot and his poetry is shit! (*The stick taps.*)

ROON (*calling after him*): Schleiss is loved by the young!

SLEEN: The young? Anyone can be loved by the young! I was loved by the young!

JANE: Not for long.

SLEEN: Not for long, no.

ROON (*running after him*): Schleiss is loved for his humanity, and rightly!

SLEEN: Schleiss has four houses. One in the Alps and three in America. How many organs was Schleiss shot through?

ROON: Schleiss crashed in his plane.

SLEEN: Exactly.

ROON: And was burned!

SLEEN: Exactly!

ROON: So what have his houses got to do with —

SLEEN: Airmen attracted women, can you say why?

APPR. SURGEON: You are vicious and uncouth.

SLEEN: Yes.

APPR. SURGEON: You are every bit as vile as I expected you to be.

SLEEN: Yes, but what is the fascination of airmen? Even with their scorched and tissue faces, still they were loved by women. (*A tram grinds on a curve.*)

APPR. SURGEON: Oh, look where we have fetched up, look...

SLEEN: No, Schleiss is a genius, Schleiss is above criticism, wonderful Schleiss, his books are everywhere and he never entertained a single reprehensible or unjust sentiment —

APPR. SURGEON: I said look where we have —

SLEEN: I kneel, I stoop, I drink at Schleiss's puddle —

APPR. SURGEON: The Museum of the Unjustly Killed... (*A wind, with the sound of railway couplings from the yard.*)

JANE: This wasn't here when... last I was here...

TAYLOR: I know the caretaker. He drinks. I know his habits. (*He beats on a wooden door.*)

APPR. SURGEON: Here the deportees stood. Some of these had certainly read Sleen. It is not impossible that one stood here with Sleen's book in his baggage. (*Banging*)

SLEEN: Not impossible. We sold 50,000 in one year.

APPR. SURGEON: How I detest you. How I revile you.

TAYLOR: He can't be asleep. He never sleeps. (*He bangs again.*)

APPR. SURGEON: Under the swinging arc lamps. Sick with despair. Sick with incredulity. Dogs barked and children whimpered.

SLEEN: It was like that. No amount of hyperbole can spoil the truth of it.

APPR. SURGEON: **And where were you!**

SLEEN: In the restaurant. As trains ripped families asunder. The ping of forks on crockery. As pistons ground down love. The unfolding of new shirts from cellophane. As rods dragged infants from their mothers' arms. The splash of aftershave. La Nuit D'Amour. Impassioné. I bathed in foam as signals flashed both green and red. I squeezed my sponge as points were switched by furtive cables. Over the frontier went the already dead, and my books stood in the windows of the boulevards like guards, like mannequins. Oh, I'm tired and slit my throat...!

APPR. SURGEON: Not yet...

SLEEN: Not yet? Are you not sufficiently enraged?

APPR. SURGEON: Not yet, I said...

SLEEN: She fears... she senses... the inadequacy of revenge... she hears... she dreams... the chorus of the dead whose howl cannot be satisfied... what's my diseased old corpse to them...? (*The sliding of bolts.*)

CARETAKER: This is the middle of the night.

SLEEN: My last, so let us in.

Scene 11

The Museum of the Unjustly Killed. Hollowness.

CARETAKER: You're Sleen.
SLEEN: Yes, so show us all the relics. The pathetic letters and the
  moth-eaten toys.
CARETAKER: You're Sleen. The collaborator and anti-semite.
SLEEN: Yes! Now hang the toys on me! I dangle, I rattle like a
  vendor, pile me with the scraps of obscure and aborted lives!
APPR. SURGEON: This is not a confession. It is a trick.
CARETAKER: I'll put the lights on.
APPR. SURGEON: I keep my nerve. I keep my temper.
JANE: Look! Whole cases of pathetic things...!
ROON: And photographs so huge we're dwarfed...! (*The stick
  taps on the boarded floor.*)
TAYLOR: You were up, then? I said you never slept.
CARETAKER: It's hard in here...
TAYLOR: All the same, a man must, mustn't he? At some stage,
  sleep?
SLEEN: I've seen it. (*The stick ceases.*)
CARETAKER: There is one other room. (*A door is unlocked and
  opened. Pause.*)
SLEEN: That's good...
JANE: What is? There's nothing here...
SLEEN: No bones. No toys. No manuscripts. (*He walks in. His
  stick echoes, stops.*) No garments. Spectacles. Or hair. (*Pause.
  ROON walks in.*)
ROON: It's very clean...
CARETAKER: I sweep it. Hourly.
ROON: And silent.
CARETAKER: Who could bring himself to make a sound? (*JANE
  walks in. Stops.*)
JANE: Did something happen here? (*Pause. The densest of silen-
  ces.*)
  Did something terrible happen here? (*Pause. The distant clank
  of couplings.*)
APPR. SURGEON: How well you wrote the three 'Democracies'.
  They praised your style. But now. (*Pause*) How brilliantly you
  articulated hate. They called it the apotheosis of vituperation.
  But now. (*Pause*)
SLEEN: I give you my throat.
APPR. SURGEON: No!

SLEEN: Listen, ping goes the stud! Crack goes the ancient collar! And the neck is like the dried bed of a river. Slit, then!

APPR. SURGEON: No.

SLEEN: We know the pressure of the carotids, and the wall's a canvas, splash the white walls with the blood of the anti-semite!
I
The
Racist
Vile
And (*He stumbles.*)
Can't breathe! (*He falls.*)
Can't breathe!

TAYLOR: Sleen prevented me becoming an opera singer...

ROON: So you said...

TAYLOR: I had the lungs. I had the chest.

CARETAKER: Contrition. There is not much of that about. Contrition. When did you last see some?

APPR. SURGEON: It's not contrition... (SLEEN's *gasping ceases.*)

SLEEN: You don't murder me. All the opportunities I give you, and still you don't murder me... perhaps you love me, you immaculate Jew? And they are dying in the hospital because you have played truant...

APPR. SURGEON: Pick him up...

ROON: If I pick him up you will accuse me of collaborating, you will say it indicates unconscious collusion, so thank you I will not —

APPR. SURGEON: Pick him up!

ROON: It isn't fair! (*Pause. The distant couplings.*) Very well. But please observe I pick him up with extreme reluctance —

TAYLOR: Just do it, you bucket of boiling flannel...

Scene 12

The street.

SLEEN: I intended to write. Why are you dragging me this way? I intended to write and I fell into your hands. That should have been the end of it, but nostalgia swept over me. What an idiot I have been. I could have been writing. This comes of encountering old lovers. Why are you dragging me this way? I never turn right at the bridge.

JANE: She intends to kill you but doesn't know how.

SLEEN: I have given her ample opportunity. Where is this?

JANE: She wants to kill you but she finds you impossible to kill.

SLEEN: So it has always been. It was so when I put my head above the trenches. And when you came at me with a broken glass. It was so when the mob tore down my house. And in the lawcourts. Always hard to kill me. Why? **I never walk in this direction**. (*The stick ceases tapping. The hum of factories.*)
This is worse than the poor district.
This is the district of the almost poor.

TAYLOR: He's trembling...

SLEEN: I take out my flask! I take out my leather flask and putting my elbows on the —

APPR. SURGEON: No!

SLEEN: **Oh, City**!

APPR. SURGEON: No whisky!

SLEEN: **Oh, we are so** —

APPR. SURGEON: I said no whisky! (*The flask clatters on the ground. Pause.*)

SLEEN: Why have you brought me here?

TAYLOR: He has gone pale. He was already pale but now. And this in the orange lamplight. His face is whipped cream suddenly.

SLEEN: What do you know of whipped cream? You're a beggar, aren't you?

TAYLOR: You see, he's nettled.

SLEEN: This was low of you. This was underhand. For six decades I steered round here.

JANE: What is it, Sleen?

SLEEN: For six decades! (*A factory whistle.*) This was my birthplace.

JANE: You said you were born in a castle!

SLEEN: I may have done...

JANE: A castle, you said, under the stairs...

SLEEN: I may well have done... (*The whistle ceases.*) The bed is there. I see it glinting in the lamplight.

ROON: How can it be?

SLEEN: Same knobs. Same mattress.

ROON (*incredulous*): Same mattress?

SLEEN: On the landing. I was born on the landing. We had lost the room...

Scene 13

A slum, derelict. The stick. The grinding underfoot of litter.

JANE: Sleen...
SLEEN: There's someone in the bed...
JANE: Sleen...
ROON: How can it be the same? This is all motorways. This is all towerblocks.
SLEEN: It is the same! Some Saxon could be lying in the posture this slut is.
JANE: He calls her a slut. He does not know her. Yet he calls her a slut!
SLEEN: Excuse me, I was born where you are lying —
ROON: Be careful —
SLEEN: Forgive me, I was delivered where you lie in filthy sheets, not that our sheets were different — (*The alarmed cry of a disturbed woman.*)
The same sheets! And the same filth, obviously!
THE WOMAN: What are you? Murderers?
SLEEN: There is some disagreement on that point. I apparently am. These apparently will be. I murdered this woman's hopes, and this youth feels his conscience killed, as for the one in rags, I strangled his many careers —
APPR. SURGEON: Shut up! (*Pause. The city through a broken window.*)
SLEEN: How warm it is where you are lying... you even look like my mother...
THE WOMAN: What...?
JANE: She bears no resemblance whatsoever, this I know because you gave me a locket in which her photograph was kept along with a tuft of hair, it's here —
SLEEN: You still wear it!
JANE: Look! (*A click of a catch.*)
SLEEN: All my life I have preferred the cheap emotions. Mother love. Children. Animals. It isn't my mother, it's an actress cut out from a magazine. I thought it better to have a mother who was beautiful, and gradually, until this moment, the fiction displaced the real... no... this is her authentic face... scarred... pale as the fish's belly... (*Pause. The city.*) Of course the surgeon will not kill me... she is waiting for me to commit suicide... (*Pause*)
THE WOMAN: I know you... aren't you Sleen?
SLEEN: My mug. Its notoriety.

THE WOMAN: I thought he was dead... but you are Sleen...

SLEEN: I live like the bacillus in an abandoned drain... Move over. As long as I am moving I can stay upright but as soon as I am still — (*The mattress squeals.*)

Oh, the bottomless depths of a slut's bed —

THE WOMAN: Thank you —

JANE: This man could once make poetry from the turning of a woman's heel —

SLEEN: The heel particularly. I made too much of the heel —

JANE: He spoke such sentences of love the sky roared like a bowl of light —

APPR. SURGEON: And hate! Such hate the little flame of love guttered like a candle in poisonous sewers —

SLEEN: Hate also! Yes! Which came in my first breath. Which came in the first filling of my lung, I drew it in with all the odours of the stairs! The fish, the flesh, the fornication! With the first racket of the city, the pile-driver, the refuse cart, the bawling of the unadored! Hate, yes! (*The street.*) Why was I a doctor? Out of love?

APPR. SURGEON: Why not love?

SLEEN: The sores. The ulcers.

APPR. SURGEON: Why not love?

SLEEN: The rash. The eczema. The beaten child.

APPR. SURGEON: Why not love! (*The street.*)

SLEEN: Love... which could not bear to show itself... hides in pain... and welcomes every evidence of malignity... I loved the sick... their sickness satisfied me... look... I carry the marks of others on my cuffs... (*Pause. A first train on a viaduct.*)

APPR. SURGEON: Do you regret anything? Anything at all?

THE WOMAN: I'm working today. (*The mattress squeals.*) I keep my frock in a plastic bag. So when I go out I am clean, and people say, she must be from the nicer districts! (*The brushing of a garment.*) Also, I walk three stations, boarding the train with the better class, mixing with the unashamed. **Oh, someone has trod on my shoes**! (*A scrambling among litter.*)

SLEEN: I regret everything, because everything brought me to disaster.

APPR. SURGEON: That isn't what I asked.

SLEEN: Who can separate the shame of wrong actions from the regret we feel at being on the losing side? Who!

TAYLOR: Give me the scalpel!

APPR. SURGEON: No.

TAYLOR: Give us it!

SLEEN (*of* THE WOMAN): It is my mother...! Look, the way she tugs the seams!

TAYLOR: Give us it!

APPR. SURGEON: I haven't finished with him yet...

TAYLOR: He can't be finished with! Don't you see, he can't be

finished with? (THE WOMAN *begins singing lyrically.*)
  Oh, if only you had stabbed him in a temper...! If only you had
  let the impulse do the work...! (*She sings.*)
ROON: The dawn... and Sleen's not dead... The dawn... and the
  bad man not killed yet... (*A sobbing.*)
JANE: Sleen...
APPR. SURGEON: Hate-caked... blood-caked... Self-pity caked...
  (*The singing stops.*)
THE WOMAN: I'm off. Don't piss my bed! (*The sound of her
  heels on the stairs.*)
SLEEN: Mother!
THE WOMAN: Thank you, I am not your mother...!
SLEEN: Don't go!
  Mother!
  Don't leave a little!
JANE (*horrified*): Sleen...
SLEEN: Weeping little!
JANE: Sleen...
SLEEN: Inconsolable his red-rimmed eyes!
  And little fists like pallid dumplings
  paw the glass!
  Her absences were
  Her footsteps going down
  Oh, her absences...! (*Pause. Then he laughs, low.*)
  Who says I cannot cry?
  They said I couldn't cry.
  Who says I cannot weep?
  They said he has no pity.
  I can cry. I can cry for myself. (*A train of wagons.*)
  Morning. And I'm not dead. (*The wagons.*)
APPR. SURGEON: Because of my absconding from the wards,
  someone may have died. A lout, perhaps. Or a loved child.
SLEEN: You see, even you have grown philosophical! I should
  have known, you could never execute anyone.
TAYLOR: I'll do it. Give me the knife!
SLEEN (*contemptuously*): You? What are you but the whine of
  unlived life? The spirit of negation? You could not prick a vein
  if I guided your finger. Now, get me out of this bed, I am forever
  stuck in the horizontal.
JANE: Don't move him. (*Pause. The wagons fade.*)
SLEEN: Jane?
JANE: Don't move him, I said. (*Pause. The city.*)
SLEEN: Oh, Jane...
  And I thought you had woven all your grudges into garments,
  fashionably hanging off the shoulder, the spoiled, the damaged,
  and the semi-stitched, the lascivious decolletage of ruined
  women, but no... (*Pause*)
  Oh, come on, Jane, they're panting after your biography, hasn't

my publisher pestered you this week? Ring him. Ring Louise, half Europe's waiting for your revelations, come on, my spine is cracked! (*Pause*)

ROON: I think he's —

JANE: No.

ROON: No, but —

JANE: No. (*Snatches of street bawling.*)

SLEEN: The bed smells... (*And chanting*)
  The bed wallows... (*And laughter*)
  Fevered
  And
  Fetid
  Place...

APPR. SURGEON: I think you —

JANE: Don't touch him, I said!

APPR. SURGEON: I think your action is entirely personal —

JANE: Personal, yes —

APPR. SURGEON: I think it is a cruelty which is not —

JANE: Cruelty, yes —

APPR. SURGEON: Which has no justification in history or —

JANE: It has in my history —

APPR. SURGEON: Or jurisprudence and therefore —

JANE: Shut up —

APPR. SURGEON: Dishonours revenge which is a pure and —

JANE: Shut up —

APPR. SURGEON: I will not shut up and you are making squalid what should be an act of —

JANE: I am tired of your purity! I hate your purity! It hangs like a suffocating banner on my face —

ROON: Listen, I think we are —

JANE: A suffocating banner and your long, clean jaw is like a battleship cleaving the air, I cannot stomach your superiority, I cannot —

ROON: We are descending to such —

JANE: She is so **immaculate** I could —

ROON: Yes, but —

JANE: **Her heroic temper**, I could —

SLEEN: Give us a hand, I am sinking into the mattress! (*Pause*)

JANE: It is impossible to like you. No matter how correct you are.

APPR. SURGEON: Yes.

JANE: Admire you, yes. Respect you, yes. But —

APPR. SURGEON: I know. Now get him up. (*Pause. The city.*)

Scene 14

The poor district. The stick tapping joyfully. A door slams. The street sounds cease. The stick is flung across a desk. Pause.

SLEEN: I'm back! (*Pause*) I say I'm back but who is there to hear me? (*Pause*)

Oh, did ever a man escape so often the clutches of his enemies? Did ever a man? (*Pause*)

I'm back! (*Pause*) I say I'm back but who is there to welcome me?

What's welcome but a façade? (*He laughs.*)

Oh, city, we are so

I

The

Racist

Vile

And (*A train passes overhead. The bottles shake.*)

Who said you could come in?

I've lost the night and now you're costing me the morning I've books to write and I'm seventy.

I don't remember asking you but who needs invitations in this day and age?

Quaint relics and as for locks.

Butter

Locks are butter to the determined.

Which you

I daresay

Unquestionably are. (*Pause. The new sound of silence.*)

How silent it is all of a sudden.

Far from my favourite sound.

Silent it was.

Before the bullet which (*Pause*)

That was

My last experience of

Silence.